My Favorite Color is
Mistletoe

Eva Austin

My Favorite Color is Mistletoe

A Favorite Color Novel

Copyright © 2025 Eva Austin

All rights reserved.

This novel is a work of fiction. Names, characters, places, and incidents are either products of the author's imagination or used fictitiously.

No part of this book may be reproduced, or stored in a retrieval system, or transmitted in any form or by any means, electronic, mechanical, photocopying, recording, or otherwise, without express written permission from the publisher, except for the use of brief quotations in a book review.

Paperback
ISBN: 979-8-9857474-8-5

Ebook
ISBN: 979-8-9857474-9-2

Published by Inevah Press
Edmond, Oklahoma
www.inevahpress.com

For my parents

*Thanks for your support, and thanks for making
our childhood Christmases magical.*

1

Audrey

The December wind nips at my cheeks as I power walk across Lawson Commons and past the looming clock tower. It hovers over me as if to say, "I see you. And so does everyone else."

Of course, Greyson chose to dump me in the cafeteria in front of everyone I know. Mortified doesn't even begin to describe it. And now, today, after a weekend of hiding out in my dorm room, my only choice is to venture out and face the music, which, in my head, sounds an awful lot like the soundtrack to a holiday-themed horror film.

Curious eyes have tracked me all day. Or so it feels.

I grit my teeth as I cut across the wet grass to avoid some vaguely familiar sophomores. My shoes slide on a patch of mud. Perfect. Muddy shoes *and* humiliation. Well, if I break an ankle, maybe everyone will forget how I fled the cafeteria after Greyson laughed at me.

I find my footing, duck my head against the wind, and move on toward the library.

My phone vibrates in my back pocket, and I already know it's Mom before I dig it out. The screen flashes a photo of us on last summer's Carlton Landing trip, her arm slung over my shoulders as my two sisters photobomb in the background. My thumb hovers over the green button. She'll want to confirm this weekend's dinner plans.

I pocket the phone. I can't deal with her disappointment right now. She's been looking forward to meeting Greyson, and he won't be joining me.

I push through the library doors and beeline for the stairwell and The Brew, our resident coffee shop tucked away on the second floor. Checking that the coast is clear from anyone who witnessed my embarrassing breakup, I shuffle into the line and rehearse my order and my game plan. Medium double espresso oat milk latte. No eye contact with the students getting in line behind me. No crying over the muffin display.

No problem.

Chatter issues from behind me, and then a voice chuckles, low and warm. My shoulder blades prickle. Oh no. I know that laugh.

I peek over my shoulder. Yep. Jaxton Harrison, Greyson's roommate, stands two people back. Other than Greyson himself, Jax is the last person I want to see right now.

He pulls the hood of his maroon OC sweatshirt from his dark hair as he chats with the guys in line behind him. He hasn't spotted me, and I won't wait around for his piercing gray-blue eyes to swing my way.

I sidestep out of line, nearly tripping over a chalkboard showcasing their festive peppermint mocha. Without looking back, I cross the library floor decked with twinkling Christmas trees. When I reach the tutoring lab, I stop by the main desk to get my afternoon assignment.

Please don't be anyone I know. I don't pause to peek at the folded paper before rushing into one of the private study rooms and slinging my backpack onto the small table.

I pace the tiny space. Deep breath. It smells like cleaning products and the markers someone has used to draw an elaborate Christmas wreath on the whiteboard.

I erase it. I'm not in the mood for holiday merriment.

Will this semester ever end? Thank goodness there's less than a week left. Maybe I'll manage to lay low, tutor students who need it, study for and take my finals, avoid everyone I know, and then get out of here.

Okay. Concentrate. Someone's about to walk in here expecting a focused chemistry tutor. I've got this. Noble gases. Periodic trends. Chemical bonds.

No room to think about Greyson's breakup speech or Jax's deep chuckle.

I retrieve my MacBook from my backpack and flip it open. It chimes with a FaceTime request. My sister's silly profile picture pops up in the corner.

Guarantee Mom put her up to this.

But I'd rather talk to her than Mom right now. I peek into the hall. No one's headed my way, so I slide into the rolling chair and click to answer. My sister's smiling face appears. She waves. "Oh, hey, you do know how to answer a call."

I shake my head. "Hey, Emma."

She lounges back on her bed. "Whatcha up to?"

"I'm about to tutor someone for their Chem 1 final."

"Anyone I know?"

Oh, I hope not. "I haven't even checked to see who it is. What are *you* up to?"

"Not much. Mom wanted me to check in."

"I knew it."

"Why haven't you answered her calls this morning?"

"I'm busy! Tutoring job, and all. Finals are this week."

"I figured. She wants to know what time you and Greyson will arrive on Thursday. She's beyond excited to meet him." She rolls her eyes. "Poor guy."

I will not bang my head on the table right now. I love gathering with the family in Carlton Landing, but since my mom is expecting me to arrive with the jerkface who shall not be named, I'm struggling to muster any excitement.

"I don't know, Em. I don't exactly have a plan. That's still days away."

"Three days. It's three days away. And you need to make one. You know Mom. She won't let up. Oh, and fair warning, Drew and his family confirmed that they'll be at dinner on Friday."

I groan. I was afraid of that. Let's be honest. It's the main reason I wanted to bring a boyfriend to dinner. "Why does Mema ask her neighbors to our family dinners every time we go to Carlton Landing? That's so annoying."

"There's more. He's bringing his new girlfriend."

I cannot go to that dinner. Not alone… again. I finally had someone to take, and then he dumped me. Right before Christmas! I clench my jaw. Stupid Greyson.

"Audrey?" Emma, tuned into my facial expressions, frowns. "Hey, it will be fine. Who cares what Drew does? Oh, and you know how Mema has always wanted to do a yuletide *couples'* challenge?"

My head pops up.

She takes this as a favorable response—which it is not—and beams. "Well, this year's the year! It's the first time all the older cousins, aunts, and uncles will have a significant other for the event." She laughs and shakes her head. "Mema's even made this elaborate scoring sheet."

Well, that settles it. I'm not going. I should tell Emma that Greyson and I broke up. But she'll tell Mom. Then Mom will keep calling, and everyone will know. Including Drew. I'll tell my family after Christmas, or at least after the weekend. I can't deal with their opinions now.

"Listen, I didn't want to break the news until I was sure, but I don't think Greyson is going to make it. He has a…thing this weekend. He's really sorry. And since I'm broke, I'm planning to work. I'll be there Sunday evening. Or maybe Monday."

I'd better get on the work schedule for the weekend. I swivel toward the door.

I halt. Uh-oh. What's *he* doing here?

Lurking in the open doorway, holding a coffee in each hand, and catching me in a blatant lie is my ex-boyfriend's roommate.

Jax raises an eyebrow, and my face heats.

Emma, who can't see him from her angle, lays into me, as I knew she would. "Are you serious? You can't miss the family dinner and the Yuletide Challenge! You've never missed."

"Emma, I've got to go. Someone just walked in."

"This isn't ov—"

I snap my laptop closed, ending the call, and stand. I fist my fingers against the impulse to cover my pink cheeks. "Jaxton, what are you doing here?"

He lifts one of the coffees. The wall clock ticks. "I brought you this. It…looked like you didn't have time to order earlier, so I got you one."

Steam curls from the lid's opening as he slides it onto the table.

"Oh." I sit back down and stare at it.

He nudges it my way with a finger. "It won't bite."

I clear my throat and pull it close, frothy emotions foaming in my stomach.

I lied to Emma, and now Jax knows. Will he tell Greyson? Will he tell everyone? "Um…thank you?"

"Is that a question?"

"No. I mean, thank you."

I remove the lid, blow across the top, and sip. The silky foam and strong bitter undertones cut through a touch of sweetness. It's a double espresso oat milk latte. "How did you know my order?"

His backpack slides from his shoulders, and he lowers it to the floor. "Observant, I guess. I've seen you order it before."

Impressive, considering I haven't talked to him much. Well, at least not since Greyson and I started dating a couple of months ago.

I wrap my hands around its warmth. "Well, thank you. It's perfect."

He smiles, and that annoyingly cute dimple folds into his cheek. He slouches into the other chair. "You're welcome."

I put a hand out over the table. "Oh, sorry, you can't stay. My tutoring student will be here soon." And thank goodness. I'd love to move on from the lying incident and go back to Jax pretending I don't exist.

He chuckles. "Didn't you look at your schedule? It's me." He lifts his laptop from his backpack and slides it onto the table between us, using it to nudge my hand away.

Oh no, no, no. Please, not him. I snatch the paper from the table and unfold it.

Jaxton Harrison, Exercise Science Major, Study needs: General Chemistry I, Monday, 4:00 p.m.

I slap the paper on the table.

Super. Humiliation abounds.

Maybe he didn't hear much. Particularly the part about Grey.

He flips his screen up opposite mine and begins logging in. "So…" His gray-eyed gaze flashes up to meet my gawking one. He grins and then returns his attention to his keyboard. "What's this Yuletide Challenge thing that Grey's *sorry* he can't make it to?"

I groan. Maybe not.

2

Jax

Well, this is intriguing. Audrey's a little liar.

I chuckle, and she glares.

I'm not sure who she was FaceTiming, someone expecting her at a family dinner. And she was hoping I didn't overhear.

Too bad. I did.

I intended to ease the tension by getting it out in the open. It didn't work.

A lovely pink has crept onto her cheeks, so I try to hide my smile. Great. Now she's scowling, and the pink's creeping down her neck, almost reaching her cozy cream-colored sweater.

I don't feel good about it, but I listened at the door before she pivoted my way.

Lying is not like her. She's kind and sweet and always seems to do the right thing. Why would she make her family think she and Grey are still together?

For sure, Grey isn't sending any regrets to her family. And Audrey's using the omission of her breakup to get out of visiting.

A breath rushes from her lips, and she lowers her head to the table, knocking it on the hard surface.

Maybe I should've pretended I didn't hear anything. My hand hovers toward her, but I pull it back. "Uh, sorry? I figured I might as well get it out there rather than let the question sit between us for the next hour."

Her muffled voice issues from beneath her bent head. "That's not the question between us. The question is whether or not you should hide behind your laptop in case I decide to throw something."

She lifts her head and sweeps her long, wavy, brown hair back over her shoulder. A pink spot marks her forehead. Beneath it, she fixes me with those *usually* warm brown eyes.

They're icy now. I make a face and hunch behind my screen.

One corner of her lips turns up. A good sign?

"We could pretend I didn't hear."

Her shoulders relax, and she massages her temple. "I'd like that. And don't worry. I'll tell my family that

Grey and I broke up. But I want to put off all the questions until after the weekend."

I straighten. "Okay. It's not my business anyway."

"Jax?" She chews on her bottom lip, and a crease forms between her eyes.

I clear my throat. "Yeah?"

"Are you going to tell Greyson what you overheard?"

I hold her gaze before returning my fingers to the keyboard. "Nope."

"Are you sure?"

"After the way he treated you on Friday, I wouldn't tell him if I heard you say you planned to slash his tires."

She doesn't respond, so I lift my gaze again. Her eyebrows are high on her forehead, and she gawks before ducking her head. "Thanks, Jax."

"Sure."

"And for the record, I'd never slash someone's tires."

"I know." I rub my hands together. We need a subject change. "Okay, chemistry final. Teach me, Wise One."

She shakes her head, almost smiling, and rolls her chair around to my side of the table. "Right. You're not failing, are you?" Her knee brushes mine, but she jerks it away.

"No. I'm here because my grade has hovered between a B and a C all semester. I need the B, and it all hangs on the final test. So a few study sessions with someone who had it last year couldn't hurt."

"Is Robinson your professor?"

I nod, and she grabs a folder from her backpack. "That's who I had. Let's go over what might be on the test. Then you can tell me what you want to spend the hour working on."

We leave her lies behind and tuck into studying. She's all business now—and really, really smart—as she walks me through what I need to know for my final.

I follow her lead and focus…for a while.

When I've had enough, I lean away from the table and stretch.

Audrey sits back. "Are we done?"

"Maybe. My brain is fried." But…I'm not ready to leave the study room. I tap my pen on the table. There's no reason we can't be friends. Right? "So I haven't talked to you in a while. How was your semester?"

She frowns. Is she thinking about how it's my fault we haven't talked?

Fair enough.

"It was peachy. You know, besides last week."

Right. The breakup. "Uh. Sorry. I wasn't trying to bring that up."

She worries her lip again. "I know. The semester was fine. But I'm so ready to get out of here for Christmas. I need a break from…everything." She packs up.

"I bet. It's been a long semester."

She nods but doesn't say anything, so I try again as I reach for my bag. "Do you have any holiday plans? Your parents live around here, right?"

"Yeah, but we don't stay here for much of the break. We always meet up with our extended family in Carlton Landing. I'll be there for four or five days. Maybe more. What about you? Any big plans?"

"My parents booked a trip to Hawaii for Christmas."

"Oh, wow. That sounds amazing."

"It will be fun. But—"

I cut off, not wanting to sound like a spoiled brat.

"But, what?"

"Christmas is supposed to be wintery. It's for big coats and fireplaces and snow."

"Snow?" She laughs, sliding a pen into its particular slot in her backpack. "Aren't you from Oklahoma? We rarely get snow at Christmas."

"I know. And yes, I went to high school in Guthrie, where my parents still live, but before that, I lived in Colorado. That's what I remember as a little kid. Snowy Christmases. I haven't seen a white Christmas in years."

"I'm not sure I've ever seen a white Christmas. Maybe once, when I was five or six. What brought your family to Oklahoma?"

"My dad's job, about four years ago. They both work remotely now and could move back, but my mom loves it here."

"But not you?"

"I like it. And I love OC. I guess I'm bitter because my parents are in Colorado right now. With the snow… but without me."

"Like on vacation?"

"Sort of. My dad went on business, so they added an extra week for a trip to the slopes."

"Sorry. But, hey, Hawaii will be amazing."

"I know."

"Is your extended family going, or only you and your parents?"

I close my laptop. "My brother and his fiancée are going too."

A crease forms between her eyebrows. "You won't see your grandparents or cousins?"

"No. My grandparents have passed, and I don't have any cousins."

"Oh, I'm sorry."

"It's okay."

She shakes her head. "Wow. I can't imagine what a small, quiet family Christmas would be like. I have like a million cousins. And they all like to talk at the same time."

"Our holidays will be pretty different."

"Definitely."

I take my time zipping my laptop into my backpack, fishing for another question. "How many siblings do you have?" For some reason, I want to know more about this girl who's lying to her family about dating my roommate. And why does it irritate me that she's doing it? Roommate loyalty?

Nope, that's not it.

"I have two sisters. Emma and Lucy. I'm the oldest. What about you? Just one brother?"

"Just one. Michael went to OC six years ago."

"Emma, my middle sister, is coming next semester."

I nod. "And was that one of your sisters you were talking to earlier?"

"I thought we were pretending you didn't hear that."

"Oh, right." I mime zipping my lips.

She's quiet for a beat. Then she huffs out a breath. "Yes. It was Emma. The truth is, Greyson was joining us for a big family dinner this weekend. Everyone was excited to meet him, and not only my immediate family. Like, the whole crew. The million cousins. We always get together on the weekend after school's out for Christmas break. And now..."

"Now, he's not going."

"Right. I mean, they don't even know what he looks like. That's how short-lived it was. I shouldn't have asked him to go, anyway. It was too soon."

It didn't seem that short-lived to me. "Wait, you never even showed them a photo over the last few months?"

"Nope. Grey never liked to take photos together. And now that I say it out loud, it sounds like a red flag."

"Sorry."

"It's okay. I'm working on getting out of the whole weekend ordeal."

"Why would you do that? The yuletide thing has potential."

She makes a face. "It's complicated."

"Well, if it makes you feel better, I'm trying to get out of something too. Something complicated."

"Yeah?"

"My mom's best friend has invited us to her daughter's wedding on Thursday evening, and she says I'm 'required to go' since we're all old family friends."

"That's not so bad. I bet the food will be good, at least."

"Maybe, but I'd rather not go because I used to date the bride's younger sister. She'll be there."

"Ah. Drama."

"And so will her stupid boyfriend."

"More drama."

"Yep. Can't wait to hover by myself at the punch bowl while they slow dance."

"Maybe your mom can run interference."

"Super. I'll be the guy hiding behind his parents."

She fights another smile. "Sorry. Sounds lame."

I meet her gaze again. "So, does my sad, sad story make you want to tell me why you really don't want to go to your family Christmas thing?"

She picks at her sweater sleeve. "Well, Greyson was my first real boyfriend. Some of my cousins tend to make little comments about how I'm always chronically single. I was ready to put that to rest."

"You're only, what…twenty? That's hardly old enough to be chronically single."

"Nineteen. And it *might* have something to do with the crush I had on one particular guy, someone we all know, pretty much my whole life. They always laughed that I would never meet anyone because I was obsessed with someone who would never date me."

"Ouch."

"To be fair, he's three and a half years older than me, which is an eternity when you're thirteen."

"True."

"Anyway, I'll tell everyone about the breakup eventually. I don't want to go because I don't want to show up alone after I've told everyone Greyson will be there." She scratches her nose. "Especially since the Yuletide Challenge is a couples' thing this year."

"Ah. And what exactly happens at this challenge thingy?"

She checks her phone. "Ah, look at that. Your time in the tutoring lab is up. Plus, I'm meeting up with my roommate soon."

A strange pang stabs at me. "Okay. I should hit the caf."

She tucks stray hairs behind her ear. "Hey, are you going to the Lighting of the Commons tonight?"

I blink. She wants to know if *I'm* going? A small ember, an unexplained…*something* flares inside me.

But she douses it. "I guess I'm asking if Greyson will be there."

Right. I shove my things in my backpack. "He's rallying the dorm squad. We'll make an appearance. Are you going?"

"Maybe."

I meet her eyes. "You should. Seriously. You can't hide out in your dorm room forever. And you can't let him keep you from doing stuff."

"You're right. I should go."

I stand, towering over her. "I'll steer him away from you. I mean, if you want."

She rises, her forehead coming to my chin, and slings her backpack over one shoulder. "That would be great." She tilts her head back to meet my gaze. "Well, if I don't see you tonight, will I see you tomorrow for another session?"

That *something* flares up again. Am I looking forward to another chemistry study session? What is wrong with me?

"I'll be here." But I *will not* be excited about finals tutoring.

She smiles, tucking her hair behind her ear again. "Bye, Jaxton."

"Bye." She pushes through the glass door and disappears down the hall.

Nope. I *will not*.

3

Audrey

A burst of cold air has me zipping my jacket as I exit the library doors.

So Jaxton's my new tutoring student. Great. Because I haven't suffered enough embarrassment lately.

I shake off the awkwardness and check my texts. Nothing. It's the first school day in a long time that I don't have a text from Grey making plans to meet up for dinner.

And he wonders why I was so stunned and confused by the breakup. Stupid Grey.

I switch my phone off silent mode and stuff it and my hands in my pockets. Students buzz about, but this time, I don't pull my hood up to block my face.

Jax is right. I shouldn't hide.

My stomach growls as I pass the cafeteria, but that doesn't mean I'm ready to go back in *there*.

Greyson probably didn't mean for his voice to carry across the dining room, but it did. I rub my temples to keep the scene from replaying in my head again.

It doesn't work.

"It's not you; it's me, babe. I need to focus on school right now. Plus, you seem to be into this more than me. I'm looking for something…casual. You're a lot to deal with right now."

My mouth dropped open, and someone snickered from the next table. Our friends sat around us, almost as stunned as I was. Most angled away, having enough tact not to gawk.

I finally found my voice. "I'm a lot to deal with?"

At my tone, he started a loud backpedal. "Well, not *you*. Any girl. It's too much with finals coming up."

And to think I was planning to take this boy (he's not a man) to meet my family. What was I thinking?

"You never said anything about something casual when we were hanging out every day. You planned almost everything we did together. Dates. Group hangouts. Everything."

"Yeah. I was, you know, passing the time. We had some fun, right?"

"Are you serious?"

"Look." He lowered his volume, noticing our audience. "I've moved on. I don't feel the same anymore. And I…want to be free to go in another direction."

A muscle ticks in my jaw even now. How could he say all those things and not understand why I was so upset? It's like we were on different planets. And why, oh why, did he have to do it in front of the entire cafeteria? I can still feel the pitying expressions from Jax and everyone else as I fled. Jax might've even said something like, "Grey, what are you doing? This isn't the place."

Whispers from students across the space followed me out the door while my cheeks burned and tears threatened.

But I held them in until I was well out of sight. Then the floodgates opened.

So humiliating.

Nope, I'm not ready to face the dinner crowd yet.

And on top of that, I'm now supposed to tutor Grey's roommate? Jax doesn't even like me. He was nice to me when I first met him, but more recently, he's ignored me. That's what made today so confusing.

Why was Jax being nice? Friendly, even. Did Grey put him up to it? But why would he?

I quicken my pace, instead focusing on the crunch of my shoes and the lengthening shadows until I reach my dorm. I fumble my key and slip inside. The silence blankets me, and I release a breath I didn't realize I was holding.

After shedding my jacket, I pull a package of spicy beef ramen from my stash of emergency food. I fill the electric kettle and kick off my shoes. When it bubbles to life, I pour hot water into the cup of dried noodles and flop onto my bed to wait the required three minutes.

Three more days. I can make it to the end of the semester.

At least I took care of this weekend's diversion plans. On my way out of the library, I stopped by the front desk to adjust my schedule for the weekend. I'm set to help with odd jobs around the library. No chance of making it in time for dinner in Carlton Landing now. And I'll miss the couples' challenge too.

I grab my ramen when it's ready and return to my bed.

As I twirl the noodles around a fork, the door swings open, and Charlotte bursts in. Her cheeks are flushed from the cold. Her eyes narrow.

"Audrey Blackwell! What are you doing?" She drops her bag. "I thought you were meeting us in the caf tonight. It was the Christmas dinner menu."

I shrug. "I know. Sorry. I wasn't feeling it."

She opens her mouth to lecture, so I hold up a hand and cut her off. "But I'll go with you to the Lighting."

She claps, and her voice rises an octave. "Really?"

I roll my eyes at the little dance she does. "I can't stay in here forever."

"Agreed." She plops down on the foot of my bed. "How was your day?"

"Classes were fine. But it would have been better if I hadn't felt like everyone was staring at me all day."

"They weren't."

"Well, it sure seemed that way." I huff out a breath, glaring at my noodles. "I mean, where are all the great guys? Are there any?"

"There are. You just haven't met the right one yet. Or maybe you have, and you were wasting your time with jerkface instead."

I snort and twirl noodles around my fork. "Seriously, how hard is it to find cute guys who will dote on us? Really?"

"Honestly, it doesn't seem like that much."

I chuckle. "Right? Oh, you'll never guess who my new tutoring student is. Today of all days."

"Tell me it wasn't Greyson."

"Do I look like I got hit by a Mack Truck?"

She makes a noncommittal maybe face, and I throw a pillow her way. "No, not him."

Charlotte deflects it and steals a noodle from my bowl. "Who, then?"

"Jaxton. As in, jerkface's roommate."

Her eyebrows shoot up. "You mean jerkface's *supercute* roommate. No way."

"He's not that cute." What's another lie for the day?

"Yes, he is. And, wow. What are the chances? Was it awkward?"

"It was weird at first. But by the end, it was okay."

"Did he bring up, you know, the…?" She gestures with her hands.

"Char, you can say the word *breakup* in front of me."

"Oh, good. So you *have* turned a corner since the weekend?"

No need to answer that. "We did talk about it some. He was chatty."

"That seems out of character. Especially with you."

"I know, right? And he seems mad at Grey for the way everything went down."

"Interesting." Charlotte hops up and starts rummaging through my closet.

"What's interesting?"

"Oh, nothing." She pulls a red sweater from a shelf and tosses it at me. "You seem to be in a better mood today."

I set my noodles aside and dig for a pair of jeans. "I am. I got on the schedule to work this weekend, so I'm all set to miss the whole Carlton Landing ordeal."

"Audrey, are you sure that's what you want?"

"Yes. Definitely."

"And what did your mom say when you told her you guys broke up?"

"Um…"

"Audrey?"

I take my time as I brush out my hair. "Well, I didn't tell her. Not yet, anyway. But I will."

She scoffs, so I launch into all the Audrey Blackwell drama updates from the day.

When I'm done, Charlotte shakes her head and grants me a disapproving stare.

"What? What's that look?"

"Well, it seems to me that you're more distressed about not having a boy to show off this weekend than you are about not having Greyson as a boyfriend anymore."

I pause after grabbing mascara from my makeup bag. Is that true? I mean, I did have fun with him. But do I miss him? Do I have a broken heart?

Huh. Not really. Especially after he embarrassed me.

When I don't answer, she laughs. "Well, I'm not sure what that says about you, but the good news is, this means you'll be over it in no time."

Hmm. What does it say about me?

"And I think…"

"What?"

"I think you should tell your family the truth about the breakup. You're not even going this weekend. There's no reason to make them think you're still together."

She's right, as always. Guilt gnaws at me.

"Okay, I'll tell them…tomorrow."

4

Jax

I glare at the monstrosity Grey laid out on my bed. This sweater is a crime against fashion. Bright green, neon pink, and…is that reflector tape?

Great. I'd almost forgotten. Coming in dead last in our dorm fantasy football league last week was bad enough, but wearing this as my loser's penalty is humiliating. Of course, Grey wouldn't forget. It was his idea.

He decided to move in with another biology major next semester. Is it wrong of me to look forward to the day he moves out and Myles moves in?

I pull it on, the scratchy fabric making me feel like bugs are crawling over my skin. I shudder, grab my jacket, and zip it up to my chin.

My phone buzzes with a text.

Mom: Don't forget to get Christmas gifts for your brother and sister-in-law. Love you!

I send her a thumbs-up, which is followed by another message.

Mom: Oh, and they decided to go to her family's place this weekend. We won't see them until our trip.

Wait. What?

Me: They're not coming to the wedding?

Mom: No. They can't.

Me: I don't see why I have to go if Michael doesn't.

Mom: He has a prior engagement. You don't. Stop complaining. You'll live through one evening. Oh, and guess what? We're supposed to get some great snow this week! I'll send photos.

Nice subject change, Mom.

I toss my phone on my bed without responding. Fine. Whatever. It's not like *I* wanted to go skiing. In *great* snow. My empty-nester parents are all over the place now that they don't have us kids to worry about.

My door bursts open, and friends from down the hall tumble past, laughter filling the room. Myles leans in the doorway. "Ready, Jax?"

As I'll ever be. "Yep. Let's go." I follow them out into the chilly evening, and none of them remembers I'm supposed to be wearing an ugly sweater. Of course, no one else has one on, so I keep my jacket zipped.

The campus has transformed into a Christmas wonderland. Twinkling lights adorn the trees lining Lawson Commons, all the way up the hill to the student center. I'd seen evidence of the lights going up, but they weren't lit until tonight.

A lively song floats on the air, and as we make our way across the small campus, I scan the crowd. When my gaze eventually lands on Audrey, I relax.

Huh. Was I…looking for her?

Her hair is wild in the wind as she and her roommate trudge up the hill on the green space's opposite side.

And…both their gazes are fixed on me.

They're making sure Grey isn't over here. That's all. I wave, and Audrey bashfully waves back. But her shoulders slump when a familiar voice calls my name from behind.

"Jax, guys, wait up!" Greyson bursts from our dorm and jogs to catch up. Audrey ducks her head and moves to Charlotte's other side. Well, at least I can shield her too. When Grey reaches us, I position myself so that maybe he won't see her across the lawn. Knowing him, he'd rush over there and try to talk to her again. His pea-sized brain can't fathom why Audrey (and many others, including me) are mad at him for humiliating her in front of everyone.

Audrey peeks in our direction and sends me a grateful smile. The two girls veer toward the outdoor stage where a student singing group is performing an upbeat Christmas song with a live band.

Grey puts a hand out. "Whoa, whoa, whoa." We all come to a stop. "Jaxton Harrison, are you attempting to get out of your penalty?"

Here we go.

He lifts his palms. "This guy should be wearing an ugly sweater of my choice. You know, since I was the winner and all."

So annoying.

"Oh yeah." Jordan, a guy who lives two doors down, points toward our dorm. "Get in there and change."

Grey crosses his arms. "If I had to guess, he has it on. He always does the right thing. Don't you, Jax?" He nods toward me. "Even if you're hiding it under your jacket, hoping we won't remember."

Utterly obnoxious. "Fine. Yes, I have it on. But all we said was that I have to wear it to the Lighting of the Commons. And that's what I'm doing. There was nothing about freezing without a jacket."

The guys argue before deciding I can wear my jacket unzipped until we get to the student center, at which time I'll hand it over to Jordan, who incidentally forgot his. Super.

We keep walking, and without my permission, my gaze finds Audrey again. She's nestled in a white puffer jacket with her hands in her pockets. She laughs at something Charlotte says. I'm glad she's out and about and smiling after what happened.

Grey's chatter pulls me back, and he's leading us in her direction.

Time to run interference. Time to lead him away from her.

This cheers me a little too much.

5

Audrey

The red and gold twinkling lights of the Christmas market beckon as Charlotte and I approach, our boots crunching across the sidewalk until we're under the pavilion's cover. Cinnamon and peppermint scent the chilly air, mingling with a lively "Jingle Bell Rock." Students and others from the community meander, most carrying clear glass mugs of steaming hot cocoa.

As we wander past booths selling handmade and local items, I scan the crowd for Greyson. While part of me is glad to avoid the awkwardness of running into him, another part is wondering why Jax went to the trouble of leading him the other way. Why would he do that for me?

Charlotte catches my wandering gaze and elbows me. "Hey. Look around. No one's staring. No one's worried about you or Grey or the breakup. They're all too busy having fun to remember what happened on Friday. Okay?"

I nod. "I know. You're right. I need to focus on the important things, like finding out where everyone got the hot cocoa."

"Now you're talking." Charlotte loops her arm through mine. "Let's check inside."

Several minutes later, we've had photos taken with Santa, chatted with friends, attended to the critical task of posting to our Instagram stories, and acquired our very own Lighting of the Commons souvenir mug filled to the brim with hot cocoa. My lips curve up, and my heart feels lighter as we head back outside for more shopping before the annual fireworks display.

Once in the crisp night air, I breathe in and let the festive atmosphere wash over me. The breakup still stings—mostly my pride—but I *can* savor the magic of the season. I love Christmas, after all, and I won't let Greyson get me down.

We browse displays of handmade soaps. Laughter erupts near the booth where a group of familiar faces surrounds someone wearing an awful Christmas sweater, complete with blinking lights and reflector tape. I slap a hand over my mouth when the poor guy turns my way.

Charlotte replaces the lavender soap she was examining. "What?"

"Jax. Look what he's wearing."

"Oh, wow. That's…unfortunate."

Somehow, Jax's gaze finds mine through the crowd. I bite my lip to keep from laughing at his self-conscious expression. He rolls his eyes, and after a subtle nod, he steers Greyson in the other direction.

Charlotte taps a finger to her lips and eyes me oddly. "Looks like your knight in shining reflectors is at it again. I wonder what that's about."

I shrug and lift a bar of tea-tree-scented soap. "Who knows?"

"Maybe he likes you."

My gaze snaps to hers. "What? No way. He's Greyson's roommate. That would be weird. Besides, I don't even think we're friends. Today was the first time I've talked to him in ages."

She tilts her head, still watching him. "Whatever you say."

We move on. The next booth offers freeze-dried candy. I try a sample and purchase a bag of freeze-dried Skittles for my sister Lucy. She'll love them.

My phone chirps from my pocket. Mom's texted, asking me to call. Oh boy. She must've heard I'm not coming this weekend. I'm so not ready for that conversation. I stuff it back in my pocket.

Charlotte scoops a bundle of greenery from a table. "I'm buying this for you."

I read the sign aloud. "'Cinnamon-scented mistletoe bundles.' You want to get me mistletoe?"

"Yep. They're to hang from your rearview mirror. It will make your car smell Christmassy and remind you there's lots of potential for kissing this Christmas since jerkface is out of the way."

I jostle her. "Char, do not buy that."

She regains her balance and juts out her bottom lip, returning the bundle to the table. After that, she gets caught up in taking full advantage of the kettle-corn samples, so I move on to the next booth and its handmade jewelry displays.

Wow. I lean closer to examine a bracelet and its tiny, muted-green stones and brushed-gold accents. It's not a Christmas piece, but it would complement my red sweater. I reach for it, and all the sparkly jewelry around me begins reflecting a flashing light.

"I like that."

I startle at the nearness of the deep voice. Jax has shuffled in next to me. The LED bulbs on his sweater light every smooth surface in the vicinity.

This time, I don't try to hide my giggle.

He crosses his arms over his chest. "What? Something funny, Blackwell?"

"No. Nothing. You look completely normal." I try to hold a straight face. It doesn't work. "Out of curiosity, what made you choose"—I wave my hand up and down—"that?"

He lets his arms fall to his sides and his mouth curve up. "I didn't. It's my punishment for losing fantasy football last week."

"Right. That totally makes it better."

"Doesn't it?"

"Um, not really. Aren't you cold?"

"Humiliation creates its own kind of heat."

I can relate to that.

He crowds in by the table. "Jordan skipped out with my jacket. And some of the guys went with him. That's what I wanted to tell you. Grey left, and I don't think he's coming back. So you're in the clear."

My smile falters. "Oh. Thanks for letting me know. And thanks for, you know, keeping him busy somewhere else."

"No problem."

I wave the bracelet I'm holding. "Jax."

"Yes?"

"Your shirt is impeding my shopping experience. I mean, how can I tell what this will look like without the flashing light?"

He reaches inside his sleeve, apparently flipping a switch because the flashing cuts off. "Better?"

"Much."

The band starts up a new song, and we stand there, shoulder to shoulder, perusing all the table has to offer.

Jax glances back toward the band and starts to move away. I both want him to move on and don't. It's strange. And dangerous. Like a terrible idea.

He swings that gray-blue gaze my way again, brow pinched. He opens his mouth. Closes it. Then he straightens, coming to some unknown decision. Does he feel it too? He picks up a pair of holiday-themed earrings. "I need to buy a gift for my sister-in-law. Any suggestions?"

"Oh, um." I lean over the table, feeling—what?—relieved? "Any of these things would make a great gift. Maybe something like this?" I hold out the green stone bracelet. "This is great."

"Aren't you buying it?"

"No. I mean, I love it, but I need to spend my money on gifts for my family."

He tilts his head. "Coming from me, maybe something besides jewelry would be better."

I nod, return the bracelet, and stand on my toes to peer over the crowd. "Come on. The booths over there might be better."

We move around the space, and I point out options as the lead singer belts out "Feliz Navidad."

Three songs later, I've purchased a candle for Mema, Jax has picked out gifts for both his sister-in-law and his mother, and some kid has talked him into relighting the sweater.

Shopping with him is pleasant, which, considering the last few months, is…weird.

Weird but good.

What does Charlotte think of all this?

But she's disappeared, so I squint through the thickening crowd and find her beyond the student center's glass doors. She lifts her hands in a thumbs-up when Jax isn't looking. I raise my palms and give her my best we're-just-friends expression, but maybe it doesn't translate. She waggles her eyebrows.

Jax follows my gaze, and Charlotte spins away. "What?"

"My roommate ditched me."

"She didn't want to be seen with the ugly-sweater guy."

"Probably. I mean, I'm still here only because my dignity is already down the drain."

"Not true. Your dignity is intact. Well, it was before you started walking around with this." He waves in front of the flashing on his torso.

We stop at another booth, and my phone belts out the Darth Vader theme song. Several people swivel my way, and Jax raises a brow as I rush to decline the call. "Uh. It's my mom's FaceTime ringtone."

"Oh, wow. Is she that bad?"

"No, but my fourteen-year-old self thought so. It's an ongoing joke at this point. I added it after she grounded me for something, and I never changed it back."

"What'd you do?"

"I don't remember. Maybe I lied about something."

He chuckles, and the song starts up again.

I glare at my phone. *Dum, dum, dum, dum.*

"Maybe you should answer."

"I'm sure she's found out I'm skipping the Yuletide Challenge."

"Ah."

"She'll keep calling."

"What if it's an emergency?"

It's not, but… "Fine."

I step into a sliver of space between the booth and a wall, and he returns to browsing to give me the illusion of privacy.

I hit the green circle, and Mom's face appears. She releases a breath and presses her lips into a thin line.

"Hey, Mom."

She's in our cozy living room, tree lights blinking behind her. "Hey, Cupcake. I'm glad I caught you." She pauses, listening. "What are you up to? Sounds festive."

The band has begun an upbeat version of Ella Fitzgerald's "What Are You Doing New Year's Eve?"

"Tonight's the Lighting of the Commons, remember? That's the band."

"Oh, that's right. I forgot. I was planning to see if your dad and Lucy wanted to go. Well, maybe next year."

I scratch my nose. Maybe Emma hasn't talked to her yet. "So…what's up with you?"

"Audrey Dianne Blackwell. You know very well why I'm calling."

Here, we go.

I glance at Jax, and his gaze flashes to mine. He's doing a poor job of hiding a grin.

Awesome.

Mom shakes a finger at me. "You will not miss the one time a year when our entire family gets together. Not to mention the Yuletide Challenge. Mema has worked hard on it."

I'm really feeling the Vader vibes. *Dum, dum, dum, dum.*

"Mom, I'm scheduled to work this weekend. I'm sorry."

"I can't believe your boss scheduled you on the first weekend of break. You put in your schedule request, right?"

"Well, I may have forgotten." It's true. I did forget. It was due Friday night, the day I was dumped. However, Mr. Wilson asked me about it on Saturday before making the week's schedule. I don't mention this or the changes I made this afternoon.

"Oh, honey. That's not like you. I'm sure there's some way out of it. I'll see what I can do."

Wait. What?

"What do you mean?"

"Don't worry. I'll take care of it. So, I hear Greyson has plans. I was so looking forward to meeting him. Is he there?"

"Um. Yeah, he was." True enough. I do plan to tell her the truth, but Jax and many others are hovering way too close for me to rehash the horrible breakup right now. "What do you mean, take care of it?"

"Don't worry, honey. Everything is negotiable. Where did Greyson run off to? I'd like to say hello, even if I can't meet him in person this weekend. Oh, and we can see if his weekend plans are negotiable too!"

Her voice has increased in volume. Even passersby glance my way.

I lower my voice. "Mom, my work schedule is not negotiable. And you're telling me you want to meet Grey over FaceTime *right now*? We're in the middle of an event. The fireworks are going to start soon."

"Yes, right now. Who knows when you'll answer again? I'll stay on the line until he comes back."

Oh man. I don't want to talk about it with all these people around. Especially since I've literally backed myself into a corner and can't get away without plunging through the crowd.

Mom cranes her neck as if she might see around me. "Where'd you say he went?"

I groan. "Mom, this is crazy. You can't meet him right now. He's not here. He, uh, went to grab more hot cocoa."

"Why don't you want me to meet your boyfriend? I've never even seen a photo of him. Are you afraid we won't approve?"

She's getting louder. My breathing has ticked up a notch.

"No. It's not that."

"Then what?"

I don't see any other choice but to either hang up on her, in which case she'll call right back, or come clean, because Grey is not returning.

My shoulders droop. I suck in a calming breath and open my mouth to speak. But I jump when an arm slings over my shoulder and tiny lights twinkle at my side. "Sorry, the hot chocolate line was too long. I'll try again in a few minutes. Who're you talking to?"

Mom's entire demeanor changes. She's practically glowing now. "Oh, are you Greyson?"

"Yes, ma'am. And you must be Mrs. Blackwell."

"Oh, honey. I'm so glad to meet you. *Finally*. I was beginning to think you didn't exist."

I gawk at the boy next to me, mouth still open.

Jax?

Mom begins gushing about his *amazing* sweater, and I pitch my voice low, barely moving my lips. "What are you doing?"

He turns my way. Our faces are inches apart.

The band nears the end of their song, repeating the refrain about New Year's Eve plans.

When Mom says something to someone over her shoulder, he leans close, his breath tickling my ear.

"Relax, *Cupcake*. Go with it."

6

Jax

Wow. Audrey's mom can talk. A lot.

But she's nice. And she seems to *really* like me.

Take that, Grey.

I plaster on a pleasant smile and keep my arm draped over Audrey's stiff shoulders. She's close enough for me to smell her perfume. Something citrusy with hints of vanilla.

Unfortunately, though, I'm sensing panic—or maybe outrage—radiating from the girl. I cut my gaze to her. A high spot of pink has crept onto her cheeks. Or maybe it's the cold?

Her fingers haven't stopped picking at her jacket sleeves since I walked over. Should I have left her alone? But she seemed so defeated. I only wanted to help.

Mrs. Blackwell waves her arms around. "Oh, I'm doing all the talking. Tell me about you, Greyson. I heard you're a sophomore too. What's your major?"

Audrey cuts her off. "Mom, we have to go. Our friends are leaving us. I can tell you more on Sunday."

"Oh, all right. You kids have fun. It was nice to meet you."

I let my hand drop to my side. "You too."

"Oh, and we're so sorry you can't come this weekend. Any chance we can change your mind?"

No need to lie about this one. "I wish I could. Believe me. But I'm going with my parents to a wedding. Old family friends."

"Oh, well, our loss. Hopefully, we'll see you in person soon."

"I'm sure you will." Audrey smashes my toe, so I wrap it up. "Bye, Mrs. Blackwell."

"Bye." She's still waving when Audrey stabs the red dot to cut the connection.

Audrey whips around to face me and glares, keeping her voice low. "What do you think you're doing?"

"What do you mean? I was helping you. Now you can tell them we broke up whenever you want."

"You and I didn't break up! Grey and I did! I was going to tell them the truth as soon as possible, and now…I can't. I have to keep it up even longer. You transformed my tiny little omission into a giant lie!"

"It wasn't an omission when you told your sister that Grey said he can't make it this weekend. That's a regular-sized lie."

She groans and lifts her gaze to the sky. "I can't believe this."

I hook my thumbs in my pockets. "Hey, I'm sorry. You seemed upset. I wanted to help. You can tell them you and Grey broke up when you see them. Then it will be done. Or tell them exactly what happened. A friend came to your rescue, so you didn't have to explain everything in front of all these people, which you clearly didn't want to do."

She chews her lower lip as she casts her gaze around, but no one's paying any attention to us.

I step closer. "I'm sorry."

Her shoulders rise with a deep breath. "Forget it. It's okay. At least Mom won't call me every five seconds. It will be fine."

"Of course it will. But it sounds like she's getting you out of work this weekend. What then?"

She groans again and rubs her temple. "Then I'll be the lone contestant in the couples' challenge."

I rock back on my heels. "You need a stand-in."

"Huh? What does that mean?"

"It means you need to take some guy as a stand-in to be your partner in the Yule-tournament-whatever thing."

She rolls her eyes. "You think I should take a fake date to my family Christmas? To the Yuletide Challenge?"

"Yeah, exactly." I grin. She's cute when she's mad. And contemplating dumb ideas.

She snorts. "You're crazy. Besides, who would I take? You?"

"No. Not me. I have a stupid wedding to go to." I'm hating this wedding more and more by the minute.

"Well, Jaxton, that would have been helpful advice *before* you introduced yourself as Greyson to my mom. Not that it's good advice, because it's not. It's ridiculous."

I chuckle. "I know. I was kidding anyway."

She huffs out a breath and crosses her arms. Wisps of hair fall over her face, hiding it from view. The urge to reach out and brush it away from her beautiful, deep-brown eyes overcomes me.

Whoa. I step back. What's wrong with me?

This is my roommate's very recent ex-girlfriend. She's off-limits. I mean, I may have met her first—and I may have been interested that first day—but Grey and his bubbly outgoing personality got the girl.

She picked him.

And I moved on.

I won't be anyone's rebound guy. That doesn't go well.

I should know.

"Jax, come on. Fireworks." Myles waves to me over the crowd. Thank goodness. I needed the distraction.

And I need to avoid this girl.

I turn back to her. "I've got to run. Thanks for the shopping help."

She pushes the hair from her face and plunges her hands into her jacket pockets. "No problem. See you tomorrow?"

Right. Tutoring.

She's looking at me with those alluring eyes.

Say no. Find someone else. Anyone else.

But without my permission, my head bobs a yes as the first fireworks light the sky. "Yeah. Sure. See you tomorrow."

7

Audrey

Two days and three finals later, I rock back in my chair in the private study room, ready to begin my last tutoring session of the semester. I tap my pen against my notebook as my gaze darts between the library clock and the study room door.

Where is Jax?

I figured he'd want to use every second of our study time since his dreaded Chem 1 final is first thing tomorrow morning. He's coming, right? If he doesn't, I won't get to say goodbye before Christmas break. Not that I need to. I've simply gotten used to seeing him here. That's all.

My last final is also tomorrow, and I'm so ready to be done. I need a break from school, tutoring, and everything else. Too bad the break has to begin with an awkward long weekend next door to my childhood crush. And of course, Mema invited Drew and his beautiful new girlfriend to our big family dinner on Friday.

They're not even family! Ugh.

Thanks to my meddling mother, my work-related excuse for missing the festivities has crumbled like ashes in the fireplace.

It's fine. I'm fine.

Jax stumbles in seven minutes late, not that I'm counting. His tidy hair is a tousled mess. He sinks into the chair and lets out a long breath.

"Um. Rough day?"

"I'm so exhausted."

"How did your anatomy final go? It was today, right?"

He unzips his backpack. "Yeah, it was okay. I stayed up way too late studying, though. I took a nap during lunch and forgot to set an alarm. Sorry, I'm late."

"It's okay. It's your hour. You can nap if you want to."

"Better not." He pulls his laptop from his bag. "How was your test this morning?"

"It went well. I feel good about it."

"Cool. This last one is the only one I'm worried about."

"Well, let's get to it."

We study for a good forty minutes until his attention starts to drift, as it usually does. This suits me fine, because our after-session chats have become the best part of my last week of school.

No one's watching me, wondering if I'm okay. No prying eyes. No work. No homework. Just hanging out.

With Jax.

Are we friends now?

He leans back in his chair to stretch. "So, I guess you're leaving tomorrow since your mom got you out of work?"

"Yeah. After my final, I'll take my time, clean my room, and put off going as long as possible."

"The Yuletide Challenge awaits."

"Something like that."

"You never answered last time I asked. What do you do for the Challenge?"

I close my laptop and spin my chair to face him. "It's silly, really. It's a family competition made up of a handful of smaller challenges. We earn points and keep score to determine the overall winner. My grandparents made it up years ago. Even though my papa's gone now, my grandma—Mema, we call her—keeps up the tradition. In the past, there have been cake decorating, board games, puzzles, a three-legged race. Random stuff. Each year's a little different. My sister thinks Mema is texting out the first challenge tomorrow morning. It must be something we have to do on the way."

"Sounds fun, actually."

"Maybe. We'll see."

"And you'll do the competitions alone, even though everyone else will be coupled up?"

"No. Mema felt sorry for me. She'll be my partner when I get there. So…super." I give a thumbs-up.

He grins, dimple folding in. "It will be fun. Maybe you two will have an advantage since she planned the whole thing."

"Fingers crossed. What about you? When will you leave for home?"

"Tomorrow morning. As soon as my final is over. It starts at eight. My parents are flying home this evening, so they'll be there."

"And then you'll be off to the wedding?"

He nods as he pulls his phone from his jeans pocket. "Yep. Off to the wedding. Sorry. It's my mom."

He stares at his phone, lips parted, eyebrows rising.

"Everything okay?"

His voice is low when he says, "The pass is closed."

"The what?"

"Because of the snowstorm. They closed down the pass to get down the mountain."

"Oh. And your parents haven't made it down?"

"No. They haven't." He sighs. "Dad's on the phone trying to reschedule their flights now."

I'm quiet as he thumbs out a series of texts. Eventually, he places the phone face down on the table and rubs his hands over his face.

"What?"

"They can't reschedule until Monday. They'll miss the wedding. I was hoping that meant I didn't have to go, but, no, Mom's sending me to take the gift—alone."

I close my laptop. "Sorry. Nothing is going right this year."

"It's fine. We'll both be fine. Right?"

"Right. We will."

"I mean, hey, what could go wrong? I only have to go unprotected into my ex's domain. That's all."

I snicker at his dramatics. "And without a mom to hide behind."

He lowers his forehead to the table. "Exactly."

Chuckling, I grab my bag. "Sounds like you're the one who needs a fake date."

His head snaps up, gaze finding mine. He studies me. Opens his mouth. Closes it.

I slide my laptop into its space in my backpack. "What?"

"What day do you absolutely have to be in Carlton Landing?"

"I'm leaving tomorrow."

"But the main dinner isn't until the next day, right?"

"Right, but, like I said, my mom is expecting me tomorrow."

"Hear me out." He leans closer, lowering his voice. "Double fake date."

"Double?"

"As in, you come with me—I go with you. You help me—I help you."

"Jax, that's insane. We're not doing that."

"Why not? It's brilliant."

"It's too much."

"How is it too much?"

"The lies are too much. This would be way more difficult than you think to pull off." I know this because I've contemplated it many times since he brought it up the other day. "The wedding would be easy. Your family won't even be there. But it's much less likely we would get away with a whole weekend with my family."

"Why?"

"At the wedding, we could both be ourselves. At Carlton Landing, you would have to *be* Greyson. You would have to answer to the name Greyson. I would have to remember to call you Greyson."

"We could do that. Easy. Besides, he's my roommate. I know everything about him."

"Nope. No way. I can't do it. I'm already in deeper than I want to be with this lie. Thanks to you. And, most importantly"—I stand—"I have to go tomorrow."

"Your mom loves me. You know she'd agree to let you come a day late if it means I could join you."

"You mean, if *Greyson* could join me?"

"Right. Same thing."

I sling my backpack over my shoulder. "It's really not." I head to the door, almost losing my resolve at the pleading in those storm-gray eyes. Almost.

"Merry Christmas, Jax. I'll see you in January."

8

Audrey

The next day, I scroll through Instagram. My thumb flicks past smiling faces, silly moments, and perfect poses. Everyone is so excited for Christmas break.

I swipe past two girls, roommates, from down the hall, hugging it out by the Christmas tree in the student center with the caption, "Can't wait till we meet again in the new year! Merry Christmas, everyone."

That's funny. Last night, the two of them got into an argument about who had to clean the sink.

Still scrolling, I find family photos as well. There's one of my cousin Will and his girlfriend, Morgan. They're like models posing before the Christmas lights.

And there's Charlotte, beaming in front of her end-of-semester art project. I shake my head. She hated every second spent on that assignment and complained about it daily.

I flip faster, photo after photo, until I throw it aside on my bed. Everyone's life is perfect. Meanwhile, I'll face Drew and the beauty queen at dinner tomorrow night.

It's fine. It's just one dinner, and I can spend the rest of the weekend avoiding him.

Packing noises have disrupted the hall since I returned from my last final. Now, a new sound carries through my door.

Charlotte is coming this way, belting out "White Christmas." I grab my phone and hit record as she saunters into the room and throws her arms wide to finish out Bing Crosby's tune.

She bows with a flourish.

I giggle. "Keep dreaming, lady. This is Oklahoma. We don't do white Christmas."

"That's okay because I'm done with finals!"

"Nice work, and did you pass?"

"You know it." She does a little victory dance.

I play back the video. "Should I post this, or—"

"No way. I don't even have lip gloss on."

"Fine."

"Hey, why aren't you packing?" She eyes my empty suitcase. "You're done for the semester, right?"

"Yep. But…I'm stalling, I guess."

"I thought you were coming around to the idea of the Carlton Landing thing. Where's your Christmas spirit? Aren't you excited to see your family?"

"Of course I am. It will be fine."

"You're not sad about Greyson, are you?"

"No, nothing like that. I'm…not as excited as usual."

"Well, the weekend will be over in no time. So, stop walking around looking like the Grinch. Let's pack and get out of here."

She pats my head, and I swat her hand away, laughing.

She shuffles around our messy room. "Oh my. I haven't noticed the mess in a while. We're slobs."

We're not slobs. *She's* a slob. But I nod. "Throw me your hamper. I'll start loading it up with all these dirty clothes."

"They're not *all* mine." She rummages around. "Oh. Yeah. They are."

I shake my head as she passes her hamper, and we spend the next half hour packing up and hauling her things to her car.

With a hug and a promise to text over break, Charlotte bounces out the door, leaving me alone with the task of packing my suitcase. As I start folding sweaters and jeans, my phone buzzes with a new message. It's Kayden, one of my tutoring students, texting to tell me she thinks she nailed her final. Of course, she did. She was well prepared. I congratulate her, and my thoughts veer to Jax. How did he do on his chemistry final? Will he get that B in the class? But I won't hear from him. He doesn't even have my number.

After I fold more shirts, my phone chimes again. This time, it's from Mema, and she's created an enormous family group chat.

Mema: Yuletide Challenge Alert! Your first challenge will span a full twenty-four hours. It's a photo scavenger hunt! You'll get points for timeliness and creativity. I'll send requirements periodically over the next day, and you'll take the photo and send it over this group chat. The first photo is easy: snap a selfie in the car when you start driving this way.

Well, that's not so bad. Take a pic when I get in the car. Easy.

Within minutes, the first photo arrives. It's of Aunt Suzanne and Uncle Bob in the front seat of their car. They're smiling and holding up a container of OREO truffles, one of Mema's favorites.

Hmm. Sucking up to the judge. Well played, Aunt Sue.

Ten minutes later, Emma and Bryson send one. They're cuddled on Mema's front porch steps, heads bent together, fingers of opposite hands touching to form a heart.

Emma: Already here!

Mema: Two lovely couple photos so far! Keep them coming!

Couple photos?

Of course. All the photos arriving in the group chat will be of couples. Because it's the couples' challenge. And I'm the only one driving alone.

I toss my phone on my bed again.

Whatever. I don't care. I'm not sending a single photo, though. No thanks.

I shove a scarf into my suitcase with more force than necessary. My phone dings as I stow my makeup bag.

I ignore it.

When my phone chirps again, it's my tone reserved only for Emma. Fine. I'll look.

Emma: Don't freak out. Call me.

What does that mean? I'm annoyed by the whole thing, but I'm not freaking out.

Curiosity gets the better of me, and I jump back over to the family group chat. My jaw drops. This couple is *not* family.

Drew, my lifelong crush, is leaning close to a beautiful girl with long blonde hair and bright-blue eyes. They're wearing matching Santa hats and are smiling like they're the cover of a holiday Hallmark rom-com.

What is he doing? How dare he encroach on our family game?

My heartbeat ticks up a notch as I scroll through the people in the group chat. Sure enough, there's his name. Drew Edwards. There are two other numbers not stored in my phone, and their owners become clear with the next photo that arrives.

Drew's mom and dad, Mr. and Mrs. Edwards, star in this snapshot.

The room spins. Why are they part of this chat?

I fumble Emma's number into a FaceTime call. She's frowning when she answers. "Hey, Aud."

"Why is Drew sending photos to my phone on our *family* group chat?"

She rubs her temple. "Mema also asked them to be a part of the Challenge this year since they'll be next door all weekend. Sorry. I know you wanted to keep your distance."

"No. No. No. Why?"

"You know she likes to include everyone."

"They don't need to be included. They have each other."

"I don't know what to tell you. They're competing."

I groan.

"Audrey, you've got to let it go. He's simply a guy you crushed on when you were a kid…and a teen. It's no big deal. He's old news."

"I guess."

"There's one other thing."

"What?" I ask warily.

"Mema was telling Aunt Suzanne that your boyfriend can't come, and she heard Hudson say he bets you made him up to make Drew jealous."

I sit straighter. "What?"

"And I'm only telling you because there's something you can do about it. Post a photo of you and Greyson on Instagram. If you don't, you know Hudson will mention it to Drew. They love hanging out when we're all in Carlton Landing. It's an easy fix."

Sure. Easy.

My breath has shallowed again. My annoying cousin thinks I made Greyson up? And he'll tell Drew and Miss Perfect about it. *And* I have to compete in a couples' challenge against them. All weekend.

I stand and pace my room.

Emma leans closer to her phone. "Audrey? You okay?"

No. "I'm fine. I'm good."

"So, post a photo."

Right. "Um. I've got to go. Lots of packing left to do."

"Okay. Well, I'll see you la—"

I hit End before she finishes.

I continue to pace. It was bad before, but now it's even worse. I can't post a photo of Greyson and me. Most of my Instagram followers already know we broke up. Plus, Mom saw me with Jax. I can't post one of Jax and me because, again, everyone knows I'm not with him.

I flop back on my bed and squeeze my eyes shut.

Don't go there. Don't consider it.

My mental commands don't work.

Jax…and his bonehead idea.

But…it could work.

But it's so much lying.

I envision the weekend again. Me, Drew, Miss Perfect, my meddling cousins, my whole family, all weekend.

I can't. I can't do it.

I bolt out of bed. What if Jax has already left? I reach for my phone, but I don't have his number. I could call Grey.

Nope.

Jax was planning to leave after his final this morning. It ended over an hour ago.

I grab my jacket and dash out the door, down the hall, and out of the building. I jog across the lawn to the dorm where he and Greyson live.

Please don't let me run into Grey.

The wind hits my face as I round the corner to the half-full parking lot behind the building.

Please be here.

My breath puffs out in clouds. I hustle toward the front entrance, passing students loading their trunks. As I traverse the sidewalk, I scan the rows of cars all the way to the lot's far end and suck in a breath as a shock of dark hair comes into view.

A relieved breath whooshes out of me. "Jax!"

The wind swallows his name, and he doesn't see me as he slams the hatch of his SUV.

"Jaxton, wait!"

He rounds the vehicle and slides inside the cab. My legs push into a sprint when the vehicle begins to creep back.

"Jax!"

9

Jax

All right. Here we go. My lonely first weekend of Christmas break.

I peer over my shoulder as I back out of my parking space and hear my name a split second before I nearly jump out of my skin. A hand slaps a rhythm against my passenger side window.

I hit the brakes as a muffled voice says, "Jax, stop. Please."

"Audrey?" I power down the window.

"Jax, I changed my mind."

"What's wrong? Are you okay?"

Her words tumble out around labored breaths. "I changed my mind. I'm in."

"You're in?"

She nods and leans against the door, still breathing hard. "The double fake date. Let's do it."

My eyebrows shoot up. "You're serious?"

"I ran across campus and attacked a moving vehicle. Of course, I'm serious."

"Get in." She does, and I pull back into my spot and put the car in park. I angle toward her. "I thought you didn't want to lie. And that we couldn't pull it off."

"I don't want to lie. But…circumstances changed, and I need you. I mean, I need your help."

She *is* serious. A smile slides onto my face. "So you *do* think we can pull it off?"

"Yes. As you said, you know Grey. You should be able to pretend to be him for a few days."

I never thought she would go for this, not even when I asked yesterday. I can go to a wedding and face my ex alone. I don't want to. But I can.

Still, Audrey's beautiful and expectant face fosters visions of a bearable evening. I like the idea of her coming with me. I like it more than I should. And I also want to protect her from whatever situation she wants to avoid.

She raises her palms. "So, what do you think?"

"Wait." My brow pinches together. "What changed? What are these *circumstances*?"

She presses her lips tight like she doesn't want to speak. When she does, I get the feeling she's leaving something out. "My cousins think I made Greyson up."

"As in, he doesn't exist?"

"Yeah. A figment of my imagination to make Drew jealous."

"Drew?"

"You know, the old crush I told you about. The one they all made fun of me over."

"Ah. Right. You know, if I go with you to meet everyone, you *will* be making your relationship with Greyson up."

"It's not the same! I did have a boyfriend. They think I never did."

"But you don't now."

She sighs. "Does this mean you won't do it?"

"No, I didn't say that."

"So that's a yes? You'll be my date?"

She's gazing at me with those deep-brown eyes, wide and bright with exertion. Spots of pink have spread over her cheeks and nose from the chill, and locks of her wavy brown hair escape her ponytail to hang on either side of her face. I fist my hand to keep my fingers from reaching out to brush it aside. She's so beautiful.

I've made some dumb decisions this week. I should've found someone besides my roommate's attractive ex-girlfriend to study with. I should have said, "No, I will not see you tomorrow" when she asked.

But I didn't.

I should say no now.

But I won't.

Oh man. I'm cooked.

Keep it light. "Ah, Aud. I thought you'd never ask. Yeah, let's do it."

She finally smiles. "It's a date. Or dates."

My heart does a stupid little jump. A whole weekend with her!

She laughs and leans across, giving me a brief hug.

This is a bad idea.

A wonderful, terrible idea.

I postpone going to my house in Guthrie until the evening so Audrey has time to thrift for a semiformal dress and get ready. We'll leave in time to pick up the gift and be at the wedding acceptably early, which my mom informed me is at least twenty minutes ahead of time, if not more.

Glad I asked because I would've rolled up right at go-time.

The drive to my house will give us some time to get our story straight. Where we met, where we go on dates, all that fun stuff. It should be a piece of cake.

I get a haircut and arrive back at my dorm room to kill time at the exact moment Grey is headed out to make the three-hour drive home to Fort Worth.

Nothing like seeing the ex-boyfriend (who I live with!) to bring me back down to earth.

He slings his backpack over his shoulders and grabs his duffel bag. "I thought you were gone already."

I flop onto my bed. "Nah. Not yet. I decided to stay one more night since no one's at my house this weekend."

We don't have to be out of our dorms until tomorrow, so Audrey and I will come back to OC for the night.

If Grey were more aware of others, he might ask me to join him for the weekend, but it never crosses his mind. What would he think if I told him about the double fake date? I don't care to find out.

Grey leaves, and I watch Netflix, nap, and then shower.

I'm weirdly excited, and I need to tamp it down. Again, this is Greyson's ex. Besides, I know better than to go for a girl on a rebound path. We're friends. We're helping each other out. That's all.

I wrestle my damp hair into something acceptable and button my shirt. Five minutes before I'm to pick Audrey up, I shoot her a text asking if she's ready.

That's right. I've got her number now.

She says yes, and I grab my coat and head out the door. I drive the short distance to her dorm and plan to go in and wait for her in the lobby, but she beats me to it and walks out.

She's wearing a shimmery black V-neck blouse, a flowy, knee-length sage skirt, and black heels. Her hair is down in soft, curly waves.

She's stunning.

My smile almost falters when a green pendant necklace glints against her chest in the streetlight. Greyson gave that to her.

But it matches perfectly, and...I don't care. I *shouldn't* care. I relax and get out of my car, and a smile stretches across her face.

I walk around and open the passenger side door for her. "You found a dress. I like it."

"Thanks." She smooths her skirt. "It's the only thing I found that said 'Christmas wedding.'"

"It's perfect."

She steps closer, chewing on her lip again. I practically hold my breath as she adjusts my tie. Her gaze flicks up to mine. "You clean up nice, Mr. Harrison."

She pats my chest and slips inside the car.

"Thanks," I manage to say before closing the door.

Yes. This is a bad idea. The logical part of my brain is 99 percent sure my heart will be stomped on at some point over the next three days.

But my heart? It doesn't care.

10

Audrey

As Jax walks around the car, I settle in and adjust the vents to angle my way. I'll freeze tonight, but I couldn't ruin my outfit with a puffer jacket. Or spend money on a fancy new one.

Jax climbs in, smooths his jacket, lets out a long breath, and turns my way. Is he…nervous?

"Hey, you okay?" I wave between the two of us. "Are you still good with this?"

"Oh, yeah." He clears his throat. "I'm good. Are you? It's not too late to bail."

"No, I'm good. I'm all in."

"Okay, then." He cranks the engine. "Me too. And you look beautiful, by the way."

The corners of my mouth lift. Not once did Gray tell me I was beautiful—or even pretty or cute—in all the time we were dating. I duck my head, pretending to smooth my skirt again. "Thank you, Jax."

He busies himself by opening his map application.

I've never seen him dressed up. And…wow. His hair is trimmed, short on the sides and longer on top. A black suit jacket hugs his shoulders over a crisp white shirt. His tie is mostly black with hints of green throughout. We match perfectly. Like we go together.

I hold my hands in front of the vent. "Haircut?"

In a self-conscious move, he runs his fingers through his dark hair and peeks at himself in the rearview mirror. "It's shorter than usual."

"I like it."

"Thanks." He grips the gearshift. "Ready?"

"Almost." I slid my phone from my black clutch. "It's time for our first yuletide selfie."

"What's a yuletide selfie?"

"The first challenge is a photo scavenger hunt. Right now, we need a selfie of the two of us in a car. My grandma will send more requirements later." I wave my phone around. "Technically, this one's supposed to be of us driving to Carlton Landing, but this will have to do."

He chuckles. "Right."

I start to lift my phone, but pause. "And after I send this, there's no turning back. We'll be committed."

"Aren't we already committed? You told your mom I'm coming, right?"

"Uh, no."

"Did you tell anyone?"

"I didn't want it to be a thing. This way, you and I will already be together, and she can't yell at me for not showing up tonight when you're sitting right here in hearing distance."

He frowns, but I waggle my phone. "Selfie time. Lean in."

He moves closer, and I smell his warm, musky cologne. We smile, and I snap away with my camera app. His cheek is almost touching mine.

Then his head swivels my way. "How does it look?"

Clearing my throat, I scoot away. I pull up the last photo and tilt the phone toward him. "It looks… convincing. Right?"

He grins. "They'll buy it."

I send the photo on the family group chat with a short message, almost using Jax's name instead of Greyson's. Yikes!

Me: Change of plans! Grey and I worked it out so that he can come to Carlton Landing with me. He can't get away until tomorrow, so we'll see you all then! Can't wait.

The text is followed by a flurry of heart emojis, thumbs-up, and texts. "We're already the talk of the family."

"Of course. I'm the mysterious new boyfriend." He shifts the car into drive.

We're cruising off campus when the Darth Vader theme song blasts through the cab.

He laughs, his eyes crinkling at the corners. "That was fast."

"Even for her." I hold my phone in front of my face, thumb hovering over the green circle. "Ready to get into character…Greyson?"

"Ready."

I tap the circle and start talking, not giving my mom a moment to complain. "Don't get mad. I know you wanted me to be there tonight, but—"

"Mad?" She swats a hand at the screen. "Who's mad? This is great! I'm so glad you guys worked it out."

I cut my gaze to Jax, who mouths, "Told you."

He angles into the viewing area without taking his focus off the road. "I'm looking forward to meeting everyone, Mrs. Blackwell. Thanks for letting Audrey come to the wedding with me."

Mom coos over this and doesn't even let on that she didn't know I was going to the wedding. I refrain from rolling my eyes. She says again how great it is that he's joining me, and after five minutes of talking, she hasn't even mentioned that I'll be absent this evening. When I convince her to hang up, Jax and I are plunged into silence.

A frantic giggle escapes me. "You may regret this. She's a lot. They're all a lot."

"Nah. And I told you she wouldn't mind if you're a day late."

"It seems you were right." Incredible.

I recheck the group text. Drew hasn't responded. Neither has Emma, which is unusual.

I shrug it off and tuck the phone away. "So we should get our story straight."

Jax grips the steering wheel and taps his thumb against it. "I was thinking that."

"I say we work one day at a time. Let's focus on tonight and the wedding. Tomorrow, we'll work through Carlton Landing."

"That's a good idea, though we should keep as many details consistent between the two as possible."

"Agreed. Let's keep it simple tonight. Does anyone know I'm joining you for the wedding?"

"The mother of the bride knows. After you and I spoke this morning, I told Mom I wanted to bring a date so I wouldn't be alone. She nearly had a conniption and wanted to know all about this girl she's never heard anything about."

"You mean you haven't told them all about your incredible chemistry tutor?" I place my hand on my chest, feigning shock.

"Uh, no. I managed to avoid most of her questions by promising to tell her everything when I see her. Later, she texted to say it was fine for me to bring you. Her friend didn't seem to mind since my parents were leaving two empty seats at dinner anyway."

"What will you tell them when you see them?"

"I'll think about that later. One day at a time. Oh, and fair warning, the mother of the bride will be on a recon mission to find out as much as possible about you for my mom."

"Okaaay."

"But you can just be you. Let's tell people we've known each other through mutual friends since the beginning of the semester, which is true. And then we started dating two weeks ago when we met up to study for chemistry."

"Sounds good. What do we say when someone asks where we met?"

"Easy. We met at The Brew."

"Ah. Also, the truth."

"Yep. Here's the story: at the beginning of the semester, both of us showed up there to study with friends."

My lips turn up at the memory. "Right. And I'd already done most of my homework earlier in the day, so I was bored."

"Naturally. Because you're an overachiever."

"Am not. Anyway, I'd curled up on the couch with my latte and started scrolling."

"Oat milk…latte."

"Exactly."

Jax grabs a can of Pringles from the console. "And my friends came in and sat on the other end of the couch and in the chairs nearby. Eventually, I showed up and sat right between you and Myles."

"And then we started talking."

"Right. So that's how we met." He tosses a chip in his mouth and then tilts the can my way. "Want one?"

I shake my head. "And then we reconnected in the study lab a few weeks ago. At which point, we started dating."

He crunches through his chip. "So what else do we need to know about each other?"

"How about interests. What's your favorite sport?"

"Basketball. You?"

"Tennis. Do you play on any intermural teams?"

"I've played basketball, volleyball, and soccer. I was terrible at soccer. What about you?"

I pop open the lid of my reusable water bottle. "Volleyball. I was on C league, but it was fun. I also tried flag football, but I'll sit it out next time. I'd rather not humiliate myself again."

"It couldn't have been that bad."

"It was bad."

"Oh. Does your family know where you and Grey went on your first date? We could keep that detail the same."

"They do." I take a sip. "We went to the movies."

"What else?"

"That's it. He took me back to my dorm."

"That's kind of lame."

"What? Why?"

"I mean, you can't talk at a movie. First dates are for getting to know each other."

"Well, that's what we did. And I told my sisters, who probably told everyone else."

"Okay, but since I'm not that lame and would do a better job, I'm adding that afterward we went for ice cream and a long walk around the trails on campus."

"Fine." My phone chirps. "Oh, it's our next yuletide selfie challenge from Mema. Listen to this. For the next photo, I want to see you and your partner with a favorite drink or food."

"That should be easy." He glances around the car and then half-heartedly holds out his can of Pringles.

I frown as the first photo comes through. It's Aunt Suzanne and Uncle Bob, still in the car. Aunt Sue is holding up the OREO truffles again, while Uncle Bob lifts a Starbucks coffee. It's basically the same photo they sent earlier.

Mema's text comes next.

Mema: Okay. You checked the box, but no extra points for creativity.

Aunt Suzanne adds a thumbs-down to this message.

"We need something unique," I say. "Guthrie's not that far. Where did you go to get a snack or drink when you were in high school?"

"Um, I went to Sonic a lot. Want to get a flavored soda? Or maybe a burrito from Taco Bell."

I wrinkle my nose, and he tries again.

"Oh, I know. We have a great local coffee shop."

"That's perfect. Do we have time for that? Your mom will find out if we're late."

"That's for sure. But yeah, I allowed for plenty of extra time. Besides, it's on the way. We can do that before stopping off at my house to get the wedding gift."

We settle back into a comfortable rhythm, tossing questions back and forth on the drive up I-35 to Guthrie. He's easy to talk to. Before this week, I've only seen him as Grey's standoffish roommate. But Jax is funny, and his dry wit catches me off guard.

Apparently, we have a lot in common. Maybe even more than Greyson and me. We're both science majors: him, Exercise Science, me, Biochemistry. We both enjoy playing pickleball, thrifting, and watching episodes of *The Office* when we have free time, which is rare due to our homework loads.

Maybe this whole fake date thing will work out after all.

I slide the pendant of my necklace down its chain. "You know, if someone asks something we don't know, we can simply say we don't know. We *just* started dating, after all. I mean, I don't have to pretend to know your parents because, well, in this story, I haven't met them."

"Exactly."

Jax veers onto the US-77 North exit, taking us into town. In minutes, he's pulling into the parking lot of a rustic-modern coffee shop.

"Oh, this is perfect." I slide from the car, and we walk up the steps to Hoboken Coffee Roasters. Christmas lights twinkle overhead, and holly leaves adorn the entrance.

As we approach the door, Jax rests a hand on my arm. "Trial run?"

"What do you mean?"

"Let's practice this boyfriend/girlfriend thing. See if we can pull it off."

"Oh. Um, okay."

"I mean, if you want to."

"Sure. Let's try it."

He opens the door for me, and as I step through, he threads his fingers through mine. Whoa. I'm so not prepared for the sensation that zings up my arm.

I glance at our hands and then back up to meet his piercing gaze. He winks and ushers me along. "You'll need to be a better actor than that."

I swallow, my heart rate ticking up a beat. Right. I shouldn't be shocked when my boyfriend holds my hand. Or surprised by the sensation of his warm palm against mine.

Maybe this trial run wasn't such a bad idea.

Because clearly, I needed the practice.

We order to-go drinks, and Jaxton pays like the doting boyfriend he's pretending to be. We hold hands again as we step out onto the porch and take our yuletide selfie in front of the round Hoboken Coffee sign.

"We should get an Oscar for that performance." Jax cranks the engine.

"Definitely." I buckle my seat belt. "I thought the guy on the laptop would call our bluff, but we pulled it off."

"Yeah, right. I don't think he ever even looked up. Anyway, we're ready for the big performance now. One more stop, and then it's wedding time."

I rub my still-tingling palm against my thigh.

Yep. Piece of cake.

Wedding cake and sweaty palms.

I've got this.

11

Audrey

On the short drive out to his family's home, I pepper Jax with questions about his high school days. He didn't make good friends until he was a semester into his new school, they drove into Edmond for church every Sunday, and he begged relentlessly for the basketball goal in the driveway.

And I see that goal firsthand as Jax navigates his SUV into the long driveway of a picturesque, modern farmhouse. Golden light from the setting sun bathes its wide wraparound front porch.

"Ah, Jax, this is awesome."

"Thanks. It was my mom's dream to live out in the country. But she also didn't want to be too far from the city. My parents work from home most days, so this works. The commute into Oklahoma City isn't bad."

"I love this style of house." It makes me think of slow days, lazy summers, and happy childhoods. "I can imagine little Jaxey playing in the front yard."

"Calm down. I moved here when I was going into high school. And no one called me Jaxey, thank goodness."

"Oh, right. Too bad."

He kills the engine. "Want to come inside?"

I nod, and we slip from the car to stomp up the steps to the front porch. A porch swing hangs in the corner, and a round table with seating for four nestles by the white railing.

Did his family often eat at the table? Did he shoot around with friends in the driveway or ride a bike down the street before he got his driver's license?

Did Jax sit in the swing with his girlfriend on a warm summer night? The same girl we'll see at the wedding tonight?

He unlocks the front door, and we step inside. Lights illuminate the space when he flips a switch by the door.

"Wow, this is gorgeous."

"Thanks." He strides toward a door. "I'll be right back. She said she left the gift back here."

Left to their own devices, my feet roam the entry and on into the living room. There, my gaze lifts to the tall ceilings.

A photo collage lines the wall, curving around the open stairway. My skirt swishes, and my heels click along hardwood as I move closer and take a step up, absorbing a wealth of memories.

There's Jax straddling a tiny bike, beaming. Next, he's riding on someone's shoulders. His dad, maybe. This must be his brother. The two of them hold up fishing lines where they've caught the smallest fish imaginable. And there he is as a middle schooler, posing with a basketball.

My chest warms. He's adorable.

This boy is a different person from the nineteen-year-old version who has ignored me over the last months. Sure, my first impression of him at the coffee shop was favorable. But then after that? Nothing.

It's like he was pretending I didn't exist.

I can't reconcile the chatty version of Jax I've come to know with the standoffish version of him. It doesn't make sense.

"Audrey?" His voice echoes from below.

"Up here." I've climbed more steps to view every photo on the wall.

Jax rounds the corner, holding a large, silver-wrapped present. He rolls his eyes. "Of course, you found the wall of shame."

I tap a white frame. "You were so skinny."

He groans. "That was only four years ago. Time's up. We need to go. Move away from the photos."

I giggle. "But you were so cute. Oh, is this you in the bathtub?" A teensy face peeks over the side of a tub.

"Don't look at that. Get back down here."

"But you're like one year old."

"Doesn't matter. Look away. And let's go." He grumbles something about his mother and her brilliant ideas under his breath.

I bite my lip. "Fine. I'm coming."

We head back outside. The sun has disappeared. He shoves the present in the back seat and then settles into the driver's seat. "From your expression, I can see I should've left you out here."

I buckle my seat belt and smooth my blouse beneath it. "No way. That was the best part of this trip so far."

He shakes his head, adjusting the radio. "Well, I'm glad you didn't see the family room."

"More photos?"

"Yep."

"Can we go back?"

"No."

"Fine. I'll friend your mom on Facebook. I bet her photos of you go way, way back."

He releases another groan.

I'll take that as a yes.

"Focus," he says. "Back to the wedding. Anything else we need to talk about before we get there?"

"Well, since we have a minute, tell me about the ex-girlfriend. What am I walking into here?"

"What do you want to know?"

"How long did you date?"

"Six months."

"Do you know her boyfriend?"

A muscle flexes in his jaw. "I know him. She dated him before we were together. I didn't realize I was her rebound guy until they got back together after I went off to college."

"Yikes. Sorry."

He shrugs. "And our moms are still best friends. So that's fun."

"Is she pretty?"

"Yes."

"Would you take her back if she *did* want you back?"

"No! Definitely not."

"Okay. Just checking."

"Anything else?"

"That's all for now."

We listen to music until we're driving through Guthrie's quaint downtown.

I sit straighter. "Oh, this is so cute. And the Christmas lights! I wish we had time to walk down the street. It looks magical."

"We can come back later if you want."

"Really?"

"Sure. After the wedding. It's not far from here."

We make more turns until Jax points out our destination, an old converted building draped in Christmas lights. Beautiful.

We park on the street a block over and cross at the crosswalk. Jax shifts the wedding present to one hand and lets out a long sigh. His shoulders seem tense.

I touch his elbow. "Hey, you okay?"

"I'm good." He forces a smile. "I'm glad you're here."

"Me too."

As we approach the venue, I thread my fingers through his, pressing his warm palm against mine.

He startles and glances at our hands and then back at me.

I smirk. "You'll need to be a better actor than that."

He chuckles and squeezes my fingers.

That unfamiliar zip runs up my arm again.

Oh man. What am I getting myself into?

12

Jax

After the wedding, Audrey and I step into the adjacent ballroom for the reception. Round tables are arranged around an open dance floor, and soft music enlivens the air.

She gazes up at the ceiling. Mistletoe, which I'll try not to think about, is strung up at intervals across the space next to white twinkle lights. They cast a mesmerizing glow over her beautiful face and illuminated the gold flecks in her eyes.

I tear my gaze from her.

No distractions.

The ceremony came and went without the two of us having to talk to many people.

But now the real test begins.

As I pull her past well-dressed guests, I nod to the people I recognize. Waitstaff meander among us, offering trays of drinks and appetizers, intent on keeping everyone comfortable while the happy couple and their families take photos.

Audrey's been quiet since the wedding ended. My other hand tugs at her sleeve, but the slinky fabric slips through my fingers. "You good?"

"Oh, fine, fine." She smooths down her green skirt with her free hand. "Though I'm wondering if your ex is planning to murder me with the cake knife."

I laugh, and she cuts her gaze my way. "You have to admit she didn't look happy to see me."

"Maybe she wasn't happy to see *me*."

She raises a skeptical brow.

"You never know." I tug her closer as a waiter balancing a tray squeezes past. "Anyway, don't worry about her. Let's eat dinner, grab a wedding favor, dance —please tell me you like to dance—and then get out of here."

"Of course, I like to dance." Her gaze follows the tray. "But let's snag some appetizers first. I'm starving."

Earlier, at the ceremony, as the wedding party entered one at a time down the center aisle, my ex-girlfriend stepped through the doors, walking at a snail's pace to the front. Perhaps I tracked her movements too closely because, after a minute, Audrey leaned my way and said, "That's her, isn't it?"

"Yeah, that's Zoe."

We, along with all the spectators, stood to watch the bride enter, and Zoe spotted my gaze on her. She did a double take. I smiled back before her attention shifted to Audrey. Zoe's eyebrows came together, and her smile vanished.

I'm not sure what made her do it, but Audrey stepped closer and hooked her arm through mine. Zoe turned away when the wedding started, and we haven't made eye contact again.

And that's a good thing.

I lead Audrey through the crowd toward our assigned table until a woman in her fifties with Zoe's same strawberry-blonde hair beelines our way, arms outstretched.

"Incoming," I whisper to Audrey from the corner of my mouth.

"Jaxton!" Mrs. Holt, Zoe's mom, pulls me into a hug. "It's been too long. How are you?"

"I'm fine. And you?"

"Oh, doing great. And how is college treating you?"

"It's really good."

"Are you still making all A's?"

"I'm trying to."

"Attaboy. I was so sorry to hear your parents couldn't make it. Terrible timing for a snowstorm."

"Yeah. They asked me to tell you they wished they could be here. I left our gift on the table by the door."

"Thank you, honey. Have you had an opportunity to talk to Zoe? I'm sure she'd love to catch up. Lots going on. One more semester until she graduates. She and Aaron broke up, so, you know, she's single again."

"Oh, uh, yeah, there's a lot to do senior year."

She eyes Audrey as if just realizing she was there. "I heard you were bringing a special someone. And who is this young lady?"

"This is my…girlfriend"—I almost trip over the word—"Audrey."

Audrey extends her hand. "Nice to meet you, Mrs. Holt. The wedding was lovely."

"Girlfriend?!" Mrs. Holt shakes her hand but doesn't let go. "Well, now I *have* to know more about Jax's mysterious date with a girl his mom had no idea existed until yesterday."

Audrey's mouth flaps open a few times before she finds her voice. "Well, it's all very new."

I start to cut Mrs. Holt off, but she plunges on with the questions I knew were coming. "Exactly how new? How long have you been dating?"

Audrey answers as Mrs. Holt releases her hand. "A couple of weeks."

"Oh, a brand-new baby relationship. You guys are so cute."

I mumble my thanks, though it doesn't feel like a compliment. Doesn't she have anything else to do right now? She is the mother of the bride, after all.

She relaxes against a table. "How long have you known each other?"

Guess not. I deliver the short version of our meeting at The Brew, and she proceeds to ask more prying questions. Luckily, as she's asking Audrey what she was like in high school, one of Zoe's cousins runs up.

"Aunt Brenda, everyone's looking for you to take the last photo."

"Oh, I forgot. I'm coming." She waves to Audrey and me. "I'm so sorry I have to run, but maybe we can chat more in a while."

"Oh, uh, no problem. Sure."

She scampers off, and I rub my temples. "Wow. I was starting to sweat under that interrogation."

Audrey lets out a frantic laugh. "Me too. And… maybe we should avoid 'chatting more in a while.' You know, before I'm forced to tell her something dreadful like how I never had a boyfriend in high school or how I nearly tripped up the stage at graduation."

"Agreed. And…I'd like to circle back to that."

She cuffs my arm, and we snag some appetizers, find our table, and glide into dainty white chairs.

I thumb out a text under the table.

Me: Mrs. Holt grilled my date with questions. It was over the top. Tell me you didn't put her up to that.

Mom: *Laughing emoji* Definitely not, but I admit I was afraid she might overdo it. I only asked her to introduce herself.

Me: Of course, she overdid it. That's what she does.

Mom: Sorry

But I don't feel like she's that sorry when she sends three more laughing emojis. Ugh.

Audrey wipes her mouth with a fancy white napkin. "Everything okay?"

"I asked my mom if she put her up to this."

"Did she?"

"She said no, but I'm not sure."

"Well, this bacon-wrapped shrimp might be worth the trouble." Audrey forks another one. "Also, I have a theory."

"About shrimp?"

She rolls her eyes. "No. That woman was hoping you would reconnect with her daughter tonight. And perhaps her daughter put her up to the question session. Maybe Zoe wants to know how serious we are."

"No way."

"One of the first things Deputy Holt said was that her daughter is single again."

I smirk at the nickname. "Well, if that's the case, you'll need to protect me."

She points the shrimp at me. "I'm on it."

Our table fills with people I don't know. We engage in awkward small talk until one of the bride's friends, whom I've known since I moved to Oklahoma, arrives to claim the last seat at our table. Trevor helped my basketball coach with summer ball three years ago and became a sort of mentor to me in the years following his high school graduation.

We say hello, and I introduce Audrey. I don't even stutter this time.

She waves. "Hey, Trevor."

"Nice to meet you, Audrey." He bumps my shoulder. "And wow, you've got guts, bringing a new girl around the Holt women. Better protect her from Mama Holt."

"Too late."

"Well, you survived." He taps a finger on his chin. "Now, let's see if I can think of any embarrassing stories about this guy."

"Nope." I pretend to wave at someone across the room. "We're all good. No need for story time."

Trevor leans across the white tablecloth toward Audrey and lowers his voice. "You know, this guy and a few of his friends started a band."

Audrey scoots forward, eyes bright. "Tell me more."

"They were so bad. I mean, like really bad."

"Okay, okay," I say. "We were young, but we had heart. What we didn't have was driver's licenses to meet up and practice—or any real musical talent."

Trevor shakes his head. "Don't let him fool you. He's got talent. Oh, but I'm sure you already know. You've heard him on the acoustic guitar, right?"

Audrey nods slowly. "Oh, yeah. Right."

Oops. I didn't think to tell her I play a little. I only get out my guitar when I'm in my dorm room, so she's never seen me with it.

Not noticing her hesitation, Trevor goes on. "But none of the rest of them were any good. You picked the wrong people, man."

"Well, there was no one else. So here we are, five years later, and no band."

Audrey props her chin on her fist, scrutinizing the other guests. "Are any of the others here? Maybe you could play a reunion song."

"No, please." Trevor plugs his ears.

I grimace. "They're not here. Thank goodness."

"Shame."

Dinner is served, and Audrey was right. The food is fantastic. We eat the selections my mom chose on the RSVP card months ago. I get my steak, and Audrey eats the chicken meant for my mom. Who knows what Dad ordered or where it went?

Even though I protest, Trevor shares more stories, and we're soon laughing. I drape an arm over the back of Audrey's chair and absently rub my thumb across her bare shoulder.

When Trevor makes his way to the dance floor, Audrey's breath heats my ear. "Don't look now, but your ex is stealing glances our way." She leans closer, staring into my eyes, and reaches up to adjust the hair at my forehead.

And…I don't want to look. Because that would mean looking away from the face that's inches from mine.

This is all an act. A good one.

Get a grip. Keep it light.

I clear my throat.

Small fingers tug at my sleeve.

Welcoming the distraction, I turn my head to find Zoe's seven-year-old cousin. She spins in a circle, showing off her pink dress. "Jax, do you want to dance?"

"Oh, wow. Lily, you look beautiful. I would love to dance."

She giggles and bounces on her toes.

Smiling, Audrey slides her arm from my shoulders as I stand and extend my elbow for the girl.

Lily grasps it, and we make our way to the dance floor.

Audrey lifts her phone to take photos.

The song isn't exactly slow, and Lily is mostly interested in being twirled so her skirt puffs out. I oblige her. When a slow song comes on next, I lead her in a swaying motion.

"I never see you anymore, Jax."

"I know. I'm sorry." And I am. But that's part of dating someone and then breaking up. All those family members you got to know, well, you don't hang out with them anymore. It's the way it is. "But I'm glad I get to see you now."

"Me too."

A tap on my shoulder interrupts. Zoe's at my side. She doesn't meet my eye, but addresses Lily instead. "Would you mind if I cut in? I want to talk to Jax for a minute."

Lily must've been getting bored because she runs off, ditching me to wilt under Zoe's hard gaze. I check our table, but Audrey has disappeared.

"Oh, come on. You won't say no and leave me standing on the dance floor in front of all these people, will you? That's not like you."

She's right. I can't do it.

I put my hand on her waist and take her hand. We sway to the music.

"So."

"So."

"It's been a while."

"Yeah."

"I'm glad you came."

I lift a shoulder.

"And I've missed you."

I look over my shoulder again. Where is Audrey?

This is the kind of thing she's supposed to protect me from.

13

Audrey

I push the restroom door open and step back into the reception hall. The familiar notes of a slow song drift over the murmur of conversations and the clink of silverware against plates. I reach for my green stone pendant and scan the dance floor. When I find Jax, my heart does this weird stutter-step I'm not ready to analyze.

Because there he is, in the center of the dance floor, slow dancing with someone who is not Lily.

And not just anyone. Zoe. The girl who dumped him to go back to a previous high school sweetheart. The girl I'm supposed to shield him from.

I cross my arms. Well, she didn't waste any time taking advantage of the opportunity to catch him while I was away.

But…does he want to be protected?

Her arm is draped over his shoulder, his fingers at her waist. Their hands intertwined. He's facing away, but my imagination conjures a smile, that irresistible dimple folding into view.

He's…fine.

I move toward the chocolate fountain, keeping them in view.

They sway and eventually turn.

I release a breath. Nope. He's not smiling.

But his gaze is locked on hers. She's staring up at him like she wants to hypnotize him. She's saying something, her expression earnest.

What are they talking about? I'm too far away to hear, but their intense body language is hard to miss. Is he glad to have the chance to talk to her?

I skewer an OREO-dusted marshmallow.

She shifts closer.

Would it be so bad if I flung it at her? Maybe dip it in melted chocolate first?

Time to be rational. I'm his friend. What would a friend do? Does he want my interference right now?

As Zoe continues talking, her hand slides to cup his neck, fingers threading into the hair at his nape. In another moment, she reaches to touch his face, and though Jax pulls back, he doesn't step away.

Something hot and uncomfortable takes shape in my chest.

But I'm not jealous. That would be ridiculous.

He shifts his weight, angling away from her, and she follows the movement, eliminating the space he's trying to create.

She reaches up on her toes to whisper in his ear. He doesn't lean down to meet her. His shoulders stiffen, and there's a slight shake of his head. He tries to step back, but Zoe grips him tighter, her expression desperate. She moves with him. Into him.

I set down the skewer. My body heat rises at the possibility of confrontation.

I'm Audrey Blackwell, the responsible oldest child. I don't make scenes. I don't rock boats. I'm a chemistry tutor, for goodness' sake. Practical to a fault.

As the band transitions into another slow song, a smooth instrumental rendition of Ella's "What Are You Doing New Year's Eve?"—I'm taken back to that night at the Christmas market when Jax stepped in to rescue me from my mom. It wasn't the smartest thing to do, but he did it anyway. He wanted to protect me.

I narrow my eyes. My turn.

No, Zoe Holt, you do not get this song.

Maybe, just for tonight, I can be someone different. Someone bold.

I weave through the dancing couples, past the groom's parents, between some bridesmaids and groomsmen who've coupled off, past an elderly couple, barely moving but holding each other close.

The hem of my skirt swishes against my calves, and I catch a snippet of Zoe's monologue. "Jax, I miss you. I never should have gone back to Aaron."

Jax's gaze locks with mine over Zoe's shoulder. Relief loosens the tense lines on his face, and those gray-blue eyes light up in a way that does funny things to my stomach.

"Audrey." He sighs.

Zoe turns her head, her glossed lips forming a small *O* before settling into a thin line. "Oh. It's you."

I force a smile. "It's me. And I'd like to cut in for this song." I shift my gaze to Jax and try to transform my features into something alluring. "Remember, at the Christmas market?"

"Oh, I remember." He winks and drops his hand from Zoe's waist.

But she tightens her grip, her voice rising. "We're in the middle of a dance."

Heads swivel our way.

"Actually"—keeping my tone quiet, I put my hand on Jax's shoulder—"I think you're done."

Zoe's eyebrows shoot up. "Excuse me? Who do you think you are? We have a history you know nothing about."

"As a matter of fact…I do. And that's why I'm surprised you think he'd go back to you."

Something flashes in Jax's eyes—amusement, maybe?—before he extracts himself from Zoe's grip. "It was good to see you, Zoe. I'm going to dance with my girlfriend now."

Zoe stomps her foot and storms off with a huff.

A shaky breath escapes me as she disappears into the crowd. I do not like confrontation. Or embarrassing anyone in public. The feeling is not unfamiliar.

Jax grips my hand and guides me into a slow dance. Our bodies fall into a natural rhythm, somehow both strange and familiar. "So this is our song, huh?"

"It is now." I bite my lip. "Was that okay? I didn't know what to do. What you wanted me to do."

A slow smile spreads across his face, revealing the dimple I definitely won't think about when I'm falling asleep tonight. "Was it okay? It was brilliant."

I laugh. "I wasn't sure if you would want me to come over and interrupt. You seemed…cozy."

"It didn't feel very cozy."

"What did she say?"

"How she regrets breaking up with me. How she and Aaron are taking a break." He rolls his eyes. "She wants me to be her rebound guy again. She hates being single."

"You deserve better than that."

"I know." His eyes meet mine, steady and clear. "And you deserve better than Greyson. That's the thing about dating. It teaches you what you want and also what you don't want in a relationship. I don't want someone who sees me as an option rather than a choice."

I nod. What did Greyson teach me? Don't date some jerkface who will break up with you in a public venue. But…should there be more than that? "Maybe we've both still got a lot to learn."

"Can't argue with that." He spins us around. "Thanks for cutting in."

I slide my hand into his hair like Zoe did. It's all for show, right? "No problem. What kind of fake girlfriend would I be if I didn't?"

His hand adjusts on my back, drawing me a fraction closer. "I'd rather dance with you any day."

I slap at the butterflies trying to take flight in my stomach. Stop it. It's all an act. I mean, she treated him terribly. Of course, he'd rather dance with me. And about a million other people.

Moving my hand back to his shoulder, I put an extra inch of space between us. "Oh, I forgot to tell you. Mema sent the next photo challenge."

"What is it?"

"We have to send a photo of us with a snowman. And she says we have to get creative since there's no snow."

He glances around. "This is a winter wedding. Any snowman-like decorations?"

I smirk. "This wedding is way too classy for that."

But I crane to peek over the dancers to spy each centerpiece anyway. "Several people have already sent their photos on the group text. I can show you when we go back to the table. Emma and Bryson took one with a snowman ornament from Mema's tree. Aunt Suzanne and Uncle Bob sent one with the OREO truffles again. They happened to be in a snowman-themed container. Guarantee the rest of their photos will include them."

Jax's fingers tighten on mine. "What about your cousin? The one who said you made Greyson up?"

I snap my gaze to his. "Hudson? What about him?"

"Has he sent one yet?"

"Oh. Yeah. He and his wife sent one with one of those life-size decorations people put on their porches. It was as tall as him. He bragged that no one would be able to find a bigger snowman."

Jax's eyes gleam. "Are you interested in outdoing him?"

"Always."

"Then I have an idea. Are you ready to get out of here?"

My lips tuck into a smile. "I thought you'd never ask."

14

Jax

I spin Audrey one last time as the song ends, catching her when she twirls back into my arms. Neither of us knows how to dance well, but that had to look awesome…probably.

Her cheeks are still flushed from her encounter with Zoe. She pushes a lock of her wavy brown hair over her shoulder to fan her face.

Mrs. Holt watches us from across the reception hall, so I grip Audrey's fingers and lead her off the dance floor in the other direction. "Let's grab our things and make our escape."

We weave between tables, and I replay those moments I held her as we danced. Her perfume, that citrus and vanilla scent, drifted between us, and I leaned closer to catch more of it.

Not that I should be noticing things like that about my fake girlfriend. But Audrey coming to my rescue was something I enjoyed a little too much.

I retrieve my keys and Audrey her purse. After saying goodbye to Trevor, we head for the door. Our pace quickens as we enter the foyer.

"Jaxton! Amy! You're not leaving already?"

I freeze, and Audrey's fingers tighten around my arm. Mrs. Holt has followed us out…and called Audrey by the wrong name. Probably on purpose.

I summon a pleasant smile. "Mrs. Holt. Yes, we're heading back to OC."

"But you haven't danced with Zoe."

"Oh, we did dance for part of a song. It was"—I search for the right word: disappointing, terrible, strangely thrilling since Audrey was there—"*good* to catch up."

"Oh, I missed that. Well, I hope it was nice. The thought reminds me of when the two of you used to dance in our living room. You were adorable."

An awkward silence follows her words. Audrey shifts beside me. I slip my hand into hers. "Uh… thanks?" My patience is running out. "Well, we'd better go. We have a long drive to meet up with Audrey's family tomorrow."

Mrs. Holt's eyebrows shoot up. "My. That does sound serious."

Oh, great. Why did I say *that*? She's bound to call my mom before she goes to bed tonight to fill her in on all the details I failed to mention.

Well. Too late to take it back now.

Audrey, wearing an amused expression, wiggles her fingers. "Yep. Please give our best to the bride and groom. And merry Christmas."

Mrs. Holt nods. "You too. Drive carefully, now." She spins and heads back toward the reception hall, her heels clicking on the stone floor.

Audrey rises onto her toes and calls, "The cake was delicious."

I raise a brow at this, one corner of my lips lifting up.

"What? I mean it. It was the highlight of the evening."

I nudge her toward the door. "It was okay."

"I can't believe you don't like cake."

"I don't hate it. I like other desserts better."

"Like what?"

"Cookies. Brownies. Pie. Definitely apple pie. Besides, the highlight of the evening was when you looked Zoe in the eyes and said, 'Actually, I think you're done.' I knew you had it in you."

Chuckling, we stumble outside and gulp down the cool Oklahoma night air. Christmas lights outline the converted historic building, casting red and green shadows across the sidewalk. Our breath forms little clouds.

I guide her toward my car, all my attention zinging to my palm where hers is pressed against it. We're still holding hands, even though there's no audience to convince. I let go to unlock the car, immediately missing the warmth.

Her arms wrap around herself, and she shivers.

I open her door and then shake out of my suit coat and hold it out to her. "Here."

"Oh, are you sure?"

"Yes, I'm sure. You're turning into an icicle."

I help her into it, and she slides into my car.

Soon, the heater's blasting, and we're cruising down State Highway 33, heading out of town.

I tap my thumbs against the steering wheel to the rhythm of a Christmas song Audrey found on the radio. "Okay, back to the Yuletide Challenge and one-upping your cousin."

Audrey waves her fingers in front of the vent. "Right. You mentioned having a great idea."

"I do. That is *if* it's there again this year."

"What is it? I need something spectacular to put Hudson in his place."

"Hang on. It's close, just around the next bend."

Please be here.

She leans forward as we zoom around a curve in the road, and…jackpot.

Audrey gasps. "No way!"

There, next to an enormous house tucked away down a winding driveway, is the tackiest assortment of Christmas yard decorations and lights I've ever seen. And smack-dab in the middle of it? A blow-up snowman, at least two stories tall.

She continues to giggle as I pull over near the gated entrance, and it's like I've won the lottery by making her happy.

I unbuckle. "Yep. Classy. Take that, Hudson."

"It's perfect." Audrey grabs my arm. "No one in my family will top this."

"I know. This place acquires more and more stuff every year. And every year, it gets worse and worse."

"Or better and better, depending on how you look at it."

"*Riiight.* So, how do we get the photo?"

She opens her door, and I follow her to the front of my car. I drape an arm around her shoulders and smile as she snaps a selfie with the snowman visible behind us. She frowns. "Oh, man. You can't tell how big it is from so far away." She zooms in, but it's no good. "Any ideas?"

"Well, we need to get closer. And we'll have to go on foot because of the gate. And be fast. I heard the owner watches for trouble because he's caught local kids trying to steal his stuff in the past."

"Oh, I don't know. What if he catches us? How much trouble could we get in?"

"None if we're fast. Plus, we're not harming anything or stealing anything. Just a picture."

She gazes out at the house. "Right."

I bump her shoulder with mine, loosening my tie. "Come on. We can do this. We get in, we snap a photo, and we get out."

She lets out a long breath. "Fine. Let's do it."

"Did you bring any other shoes?"

"Uh. No. But my heels aren't that tall. It should be fine."

I toss my tie in the back seat. "Ready?"

"Um…yeah?"

"Is that a question?"

She watches the place on my cheek where my dimple folds in. She rolls her eyes. "No. It's not a question. Come on." Grabbing my sleeve, she pulls me along and through a gap in the gate. We stick to the shadows, avoiding the driveway and the red and green lights lining it. We dart from tree to tree until we're at the edge of the yard. We squat beside a tree.

"There's no avoiding the light in there, but for the best photo, we need to get near the base of the snowman."

"We'll have to make a run for it."

She gives a sharp nod. "Now?"

"Now."

Crouching, we weave around Santas, nutcrackers, a blow-up Grinch, and even a small working roller coaster. Lights twinkle in Rudolph's nose, on an elf, around a giant candy cane, and basically in every direction.

Then the massive snowman looms over us, its eyes seeming to follow our movement.

"Here." She positions us in front of the inflatable giant.

I step close and catch another whiff of her perfume. She extends her arm toward the ground for an upward-facing selfie, and I lean in, my cheek pressing against hers. Frosty smiles overhead.

"Say Christmas cookies," she whispers.

"Christmas cookies."

She snaps several wide-zoom shots, adjusting the angle with each one.

A muffled, high-pitched bark cuts through the night.

We freeze, cheek to cheek.

The creak of a door and a second bark, louder this time.

"Uh-oh." I turn back toward the house. A tiny ball of fur, some terrier in a Christmas sweater, is charging down the front porch steps. The porch light flips on. "Run!"

We dart back into the trees, and the yappy dog follows us all the way to the main road. There, he stops feet from the gate. He trots across the pavement, barking as if to say, "Look what I did."

"Who's out there?" a gruff voice calls.

The dog wags its tail, and we don't stick around to answer. Laughing and breathless, we sprint to my car. I fumble the keys from my pocket. The doors unlock, and we tumble inside, slamming them behind us.

"Drive, drive, drive." Audrey gasps between fits of giggles.

I swerve back onto the road with more speed than necessary. The homeowner is peering out his front door, and the victorious pooch is prancing back up the driveway.

Once we're safely around the corner, Audrey collapses against the seat, still giggling. "We were put in our place by the smallest guard dog ever."

I veer onto a side street and pull over to catch my breath. "And he was wearing a Christmas sweater. Humiliating. I'll never be able to show my face around town again. Did we get the photo?"

She unlocks her phone and bursts into another fit of laughter.

"What?"

"Look."

There we are, cheeks pressed together, grinning like idiots in front of the giant snowman. I seem happier than I've felt in months. In one of the shots, the house is visible in the background. The mini dog balances on its back legs, peering out a lit-up window.

I chuckle. "When we tell this story, we should make the dog out to be bigger and much more vicious."

She swipes through her photos. She's captured more shots of us running. They're mostly blurry, but in one, you can see the Christmas guard dog hot on our heels.

She giggles again. "This calls for a two-photo submission." She edits the first photo by circling the dog in the window and then sends our double photo adventure on the group chat.

I start driving, and her phone starts buzzing. As I navigate Guthrie's softly lit streets, she reads aloud.

"'Oh my goodness. Dying.' That's from my sister Lucy. 'Where in the world did you find this yard?' That's Dad. And from Mema, ten points to Audrey and her young man. Setting the bar high!"

"Young man?" I raise an eyebrow. "Makes me sound like I'm twelve."

"That's just Mema-speak. Oh, Morgan and Will found a yard with two inflatable snowmen. But they're regular-sized. No competition."

Audrey's cheeks are still flushed from our escapade, her hair is wild, and her eyes are bright. There's something so beautiful about her excitement that I almost forget this is all fake.

Her phone pings with a new message, and Audrey stares at the screen, her expression shifting.

"What is it? Did someone find a bigger snowman?"

"No, it's from Mema." Her voice comes across careful. "It's the next challenge."

I wait for her to elaborate, but she continues to stare at her phone, biting her lower lip.

"And? What is it?"

Audrey slips her phone into her purse. "We need to take a photo in front of Christmas lights."

Something about her tone says there's more to it. "That's it? Just Christmas lights? That's too easy after the snowman heist."

"Yep, just the lights." She meets my gaze. "Let's go through downtown before we head back. The lights there will be perfect."

I follow her instructions, but she's not telling me something.

15

Audrey

I pull Jax's suit jacket tighter around me, and, not for
the first time, discreetly inhale the remnants of his
woodsy cologne. I don't hate it.

The dashboard lights cast a soft blue glow across his
face as he drives, highlighting his jawline and that
ridiculous dimple that appears each time he smiles.

But the smile has faded, though it's not quite a
frown, either. His gaze keeps bouncing to me. He
knows I'm keeping something from him, but I *will not*
tell him the whole of the photo challenge. The
Christmas-lights part is fine and true enough, but the
rest? It's too much for a fake date.

My toe taps a nervous rhythm on the floor mats, and my fingers can't stop fidgeting with my necklace.

"So…" Jax's thumbs drum against the steering wheel as we cruise back toward town. He opens his mouth like he's about to say something, closes it, and seems to settle on something else. "For tomorrow, do I need multiple pet names for you? Or should I stick with Cupcake?"

My shoulders relax. "You can't call me Cupcake. That's what Mom calls me."

"She and I could totally bond over the mutual endearment."

I tap my lip, pretending to contemplate. "Nope. And what should I call you? Baby? Honeybun? Darlin'?"

He makes a face. "Yeah, maybe we forget the nicknames."

"Agreed. How about more get-to-know-you questions? Basic stuff a couple should know about each other."

"Good idea. You go first."

"Okay, um, what's your favorite fast-food restaurant?"

"Qdoba. I can eat Mexican food any day. You?"

"Same."

"Really?"

"Yeah. I spend way too much money there."

We share more favorites as we approach downtown Guthrie, where Christmas lights appear in shop windows and wrap around lampposts.

I slide my pendant along its thin chain, a deeper question slipping from my lips. "So…how was it seeing your ex tonight?"

Jax's expression shifts, a tightness crimping the skin around his eyes. "It was awkward. Weird. I'm glad to have it out of the way."

"Did it make you sad?"

"No, not at all. In fact, it helped me to know I'm over her. I don't want to date her again, even if it's on the table."

"Because it is on the table. I heard her."

"Well, not anymore. That was before my tough-as-nails girlfriend told her to back off." He chuckles. "She wanted to give it another chance. I said no."

This gives me way more pleasure than it should.

He signals to pull into a parking spot along the street. "How are you doing since your breakup?"

"Is it weird if I say I haven't thought about it much today?" A bitter laugh escapes. "I was more humiliated by the public breakup than anything. But the rejection still stings."

"Does it still make you sad?"

I lift a shoulder. "Not much."

He shifts into park and swallows. "And would you take him back if he asked?"

"No, probably not."

"Probably not?"

"Definitely not?"

He unbuckles. "Well, I'm glad you're feeling better. Like I said before, you deserve better."

My cheeks warm under his gaze. "Thank you."

I slide the stone, still clamped between my fingers, down the chain again.

He tracks the movement. "He gave you that, right?"

My hand stills, and my eyebrows shoot up. "How did you know Grey gave me this?"

Jax turns in his seat. "I, uh, saw it before he took you out for your birthday that night. Is it special to you?"

"No, not anymore. Though it's like the only thoughtful thing he ever did for me. I pointed it out at an antique store about a month before my birthday. Oh, you were there. It was that time a big group of us went shopping in downtown Edmond and ate lunch at The Mule. Anyway, it wasn't expensive or anything. But I liked it, and I was shocked he gave it to me. That he actually remembered after all that time." I slide it to the other end of the chain. "I didn't even think he was listening when I showed him."

Jax clears his throat. "Audrey, I—" He swallows, turning his attention out the window. "Never mind."

I grab his sleeve as he reaches for the door handle. "Jaxton, what?"

He sinks back into his seat. "I shouldn't tell you."

"Tell me what? Is it about my necklace?"

"Yeah, but—"

"Please tell me."

He sighs. "Okay, but only because he deserves it for embarrassing you the way he did."

"Okaaay."

"Grey didn't remember the necklace. It was me."

"What?" The word comes out barely above a whisper.

Jax's cheeks flush in the dim light, and he stares at the pendant. "The day before your birthday, Charlotte asked Grey what he was getting you. He'd forgotten, but he still had time. The next day, while Grey was in class, he texted, saying he still didn't have anything for you and he wouldn't have time before you went out to dinner that evening. He begged me to get you something. Anything. I admit I was annoyed he couldn't manage to be a better boyfriend, but I remembered the necklace and knew you'd love it. So I drove downtown and bought it. I had it wrapped at the store and gave it to him right before he met you for dinner."

He lifts his head and meets my gaze. My jaw has slackened, and I can't find any words. He can't be serious. This was Grey's one redeeming act. The thing I hung onto during all the times he wasn't there for me.

I drop the pendant against my chest and find my voice. "Are you telling me the one sweet thing Grey did for me wasn't from him at all? It was you."

"Um, yes?"

"Seriously, he's the worst. Why didn't anyone tell me? Why didn't *you* tell me?"

"I'm sorry. I should have kept this to myself."

I fidget with the buttons on his coat sleeve. "No, I—I just feel embarrassed all over again."

"There's no reason to be embarrassed. You didn't do anything wrong. He's the one who didn't treat you the way you deserved."

I touch the pendant again, seeing it differently now. "Why would you do that? Drive all the way over there to get this? You could have gotten anything."

Jax runs a hand through his hair. "You seemed excited about it. Grey was being Grey. I don't know. It was your birthday, and you deserved something great."

Those stormy gray-blue eyes stare at me, and something in my chest flip-flops along with my opinion of Jax. He pays attention. He's thoughtful. And he's nice.

But…he did ignore me for a long time. I still can't make sense of it.

I shake my head and snug his jacket close, covering the necklace. "Maybe I shouldn't have worn it after the breakup. I could regift it to one of my sisters."

Jax doesn't smile at my attempt to lighten the mood, but his voice is soft. "It suits you. You should keep it if you like it."

His head angles toward the light-lined street. How many other kind things has he done in the background that I never noticed? I grip the pendant in my fist. Maybe it is special to me after all. "I do like it."

He grins, that dimple threatening to appear. "Well, there you go."

I smile back, cheeks warming under his scrutiny, so I reach for the door handle. "Ready for the next photo?"

"Ready. Uh, remind me what we're taking a photo of."

I climb from the car, and the December air slaps me. I snuggle deeper into Jax's jacket. "We need a selfie in front of great Christmas lights." In this section of downtown, lights crisscross over the road, creating a canopy of twinkling stars. Garlands drape every lamppost, and each storefront competes to have the most festive display. It's right out of a Hallmark movie. "And this is perfect."

We walk down the sidewalk, close but not touching. I scan for the perfect spot to capture the most lights. Small-town Guthrie is dead at this time of night. Shops are closed, and few cars line the street.

I pull Jax toward me on the sidewalk, putting the best lights behind us, and extend my camera.

"Ready?"

He leans in, and I snap a picture and then review it. The corners of my lips turn down. "It's nice, but…how about you kiss me on the cheek? It might win brownie points with Mema."

He shrugs. "Okay."

I extend my arm, and his lips are warm against my cold skin. Something flutters in my chest, that little flip-flop I choose to ignore as I snap several shots. I open my photo app to examine them, and he peers over my shoulder. Good enough. I switch to the group text.

Mema's original challenge will be far up the feed. Several new photos have appeared: Mom and Dad kissing in front of the Meeting House, Aunt Suzanne and Uncle Bob sharing a sloppy kiss by Mema's Christmas tree. Gross. And, yep, she's clutching the snowman tin of OREO truffles.

Jax chuckles behind me.

I send our photo.

Within seconds, my phone buzzes with responses, including three thumbs-down emojis.

"You can do better than that, Grey," my cousin Hudson texts.

Mema's says, "I take your ten points back."

I close the messages, but not quickly enough.

"Uh, what was that? What did we do wrong?"

"No, it's fine. It's nothing." I shove my phone in my pocket.

"Audrey, someone told me—well, Grey—that I could have done better. That's not nothing."

"It is nothing. It's fine. I'm freezing. Let's head back —"

His eyebrows shoot high on his forehead. "Oh."

"What?"

He meets my gaze, and his lips twitch up. "We're supposed to kiss, aren't we?"

My shoulders droop. "Um, maybe."

His eyes crinkle at the corners. "Why didn't you tell me?"

I groan. "Oh, lots of reasons. One being that my family is beyond weird. Whose family sends kissing photos over a group text?" I raise my hand. "That would be mine. And, two, I didn't want you to feel any pressure to kiss me because my mema challenged you to."

He's still grinning, his thumbs hooked in his pockets, devastatingly handsome in his white button-down shirt.

I cross my arms. "Stop smiling already." My fingers reach up to grip the pendant. "And, three, I was too nervous to tell you." Or kiss you. But I don't say this out loud.

He steps closer and crosses his arms. "Yes, it's weird. But my family does weird stuff too. I mean, I'm about to pretend to be my roommate. That has weird written all over it. And two, you don't need to be nervous to tell me the truth about something like that. We can decide this stuff together since we're in it together." He holds up three fingers. "And three, I don't feel pressure to kiss you because your mema challenged me to. I *want* to kiss you because…because my cheek-kiss and I were called into question."

A nervous laugh escapes me, not only because he's funny but also because he said the words *I want to kiss you*. "Jaxton, you don't have to kiss me."

"Oh, we're kissing. My reputation is on the line here."

I raise an eyebrow.

Catching his demand, he backpedals. "If you agree to it, of course."

I rub my forehead. "This is crazy."

"Is that a yes?"

"Well, I guess, since your reputation is on the line."

"Good. Okay. Let's kiss then."

My pulse ticks up a notch. "Okay. So I'll—" I loop an arm over his shoulder, his rapid heartbeat thrumming against my side. I extend my phone with the other arm and glance his way. Why am I so nervous?

His arm comes around my back. "Ready."

"Yep."

We lean together, and his lips press against mine for a nice, albeit awkward, moment.

There. Done.

I step back, and Jax is still gazing at me.

He clears his throat, glancing down at my phone. "How's the photo?"

"Um."

"What?"

"I forgot to take it."

"Are you serious?"

I open the photo app, and sure enough. No kissing photo.

He chuckles. "Uh, Cupcake, what happened there?"

"I don't know! I was nervous. I didn't expect it to be so—" I press my lips into a thin line.

"What? Please don't say 'bad.'"

I chew on my lip. "No, definitely not bad."

His grin is back, and he takes my phone. "Mind if I take it this time?"

"Be my guest."

He grabs my hand and tugs me to the edge of the sidewalk, looking both ways. "I have an idea."

"Another one?"

"Yes. And it's as good as the first."

We wait for a car to mosey past. When the street is empty again, he tugs me into the middle of the road, where the lights and the buildings will be symmetrical on either side of us. Neither of us says anything as he adjusts the zoom on my phone to .5 and slides an arm around my waist. I rise on my toes to drape an arm over his shoulders while my other hand moves to his chest below his collar. He extends his arm with my camera, and I follow the movement. My pulse hits overdrive when we both turn away from the phone, and our gazes lock.

Without a word, we close the gap between us, our lips coming together, soft and tentative at first, then with more confidence. My eyes flutter closed, and I lean into him. My hand begins to slide over his collar, but a door slams down the street. We break apart, breathless when another car rounds the corner ahead and headlights blind us.

"Come on." Jax grabs my hand and hauls me back onto the sidewalk. We pause, our breaths coming fast, the air between us charged with something I never felt with Grey. Jax's eyes are bright as he steps closer. Will he…kiss me again?

But then, his eyes clear, and he shakes his head.

I squeeze his fingers. "How's the photo? Was it worth nearly getting run over?"

Before he can pull up our perfect photo, he says, "Oh, it was."

16

Jax

I can't stop tapping my fingers against the worn leather armrest. The dorm lobby is empty—just me, my duffel bag, and the memory of last night's kiss playing on repeat in my head.

It wasn't supposed to feel so…real. A fake kiss for a fake relationship. So why am I still thinking about it?

Well, that would be because it didn't seem all that fake at all.

I rub my temple. "And because you like her, you idiot."

There, I said it out loud. I like my roommate's very recent ex-girlfriend.

What is wrong with me?

This was all supposed to be straightforward. She helps me by accompanying me to the wedding, and I help her by pretending to be Greyson. Simple.

But this is way past simple. I can't stop my feelings for her. And she seemed as stunned as I was after the kiss last night. Or is that me hoping she was? Was it simply part of an act?

Only…there was no audience.

But she did say she wouldn't go back to Grey even if he wanted to get back together.

Is there a chance she could feel the same?

Ugh. This is not good. I totally have a crush on a girl who is pretending to like me. And we'll be spending the next two days together. How am I supposed to navigate this? How will I ever know what's real and what's not?

I shouldn't have kissed her.

And I shouldn't have told her I'm the one who bought the necklace. It shows just how aware I was of her. Am aware of her. But Grey shouldn't get credit for something so perfect.

So, how do I keep from liking her?

I rub my palms on my thighs and stand. Pacing the room, I check my phone. Audrey's running late. Is she as keyed up about a two-and-a-half-hour drive as I am?

Movement catches my eye. Audrey's teal Mini Cooper—which I'm excited to fold myself into for a long drive—is pulling in the parking lot.

I grab my bag and step outside. She waves and smiles that alluring smile.

I don't *want* to keep from liking her.

Oh man.

I wave back, my own dopey grin in place, and crunch in.

Huh. The Mini isn't *that* cramped.

The warmth of the heater and the faint scent of cinnamon welcome me. Audrey sits behind the wheel, her hair in a messy bun, while loose, wavy strands frame her face. Her pink, red, and white sweater says festive without being over the top. The necklace I bought her rests around her neck.

She's still smiling, her cheeks showing a hint of pink. Yep. She's thinking about the kiss too. This brightens my mood way more than it should.

"Hey." My voice comes out softer than intended.

"Hey, yourself. Sorry, I'm late."

"No problem. I was hanging out in the lobby."

"Anyone else still around?"

"Nope. Just me."

"My dorm was dead too." She glances at my gray pullover. "I'm surprised you didn't wear the ugly sweater. You know how much my mom loves it."

"Are you kidding? I burned it."

"What?"

"Not really. But I did get rid of it as soon as possible."

"Too bad."

I inhale through my nose. "Smells good in here."

"Thanks. I'm not sure why it smells like cinnamon." She looks around in the back seat. "I don't have anything cinnamon in the car. It's weird."

An awkward silence settles between us as we make our way to the highway. We talked all afternoon yesterday, but now it's like we're back where we started.

We're two people connected by my roommate.

And one great kiss I'm not sure how to process.

Audrey merges her toy-sized car onto the highway. "It's a long drive. You can nap if you want. I can wake you in an hour to go over everything again."

"I'm good." I fiddle with the seat belt. "Did you tell your family we're on our way?"

"I did. Everyone's excited to meet you." She pauses. "Well, to meet Greyson."

"Right." Greyson.

"I should practice using your alias...Grey."

"This is going to be weird."

"Yeah." She white-knuckle grips the steering wheel.

"Nervous?"

She lets out a soft laugh. "Maybe."

"Me too. A little."

We merge onto the highway, and the tension between us eases as miles of Oklahoma farmland roll by.

"My cousin Will distributed a playlist for the trip." She already has it displayed on her phone. "Hope you can handle country music. It's not what we always listen to, but the small-town vibes bring it out in us. And I'll bet there are some old Christmas songs on here too."

"I'm in. Music and all."

"Good." She starts up the first song, and sure enough, it's a country Christmas mash-up. "Told ya. So, have you ever been to Carlton Landing?"

"No, but I've heard of it."

Her face lights up. "Oh, you'll love it. It's right on Lake Eufaula, and everything is close enough to walk to. I'll give you the tour tomorrow."

Her enthusiasm warms me.

"My parents bought the house where we'll be staying, but Mema lives there now. And my sister Emma has lived there since the end of last summer. But, as I said, she'll be with us at OC next semester. Anyway, ever since my cousin Hudson and his wife, Ava, got engaged in Carlton Landing, Mema believes it's the perfect place for romance." She rolls her eyes, but a fondness softens her voice. She reaches up, pushing the button to open the shade covering her sunroof. "I guess that's been true for some people. Since my papa died, Mema's taken it upon herself to be the family matchmaker and romance expert."

She yelps as a tiny bundle falls from the now-open space. "What is that?"

It hangs between us before plopping to the console.

I pick it up and turn it over in my hands. "Um, did you forget you had a handful of mistletoe hidden in the sunroof?"

Her mouth drops open, and her cheeks glow an appealing shade of pink. She grabs it from my hands, as a muscle ticks in her jaw. "Charlotte! She must have snuck it in here."

I chuckle. "Why?"

"To make my car smell Christmassy, and—" She cuts her gaze to me. "It's to hang from your rearview mirror. She is so on the naughty list. I told her not to buy it."

She starts to roll down her window to throw it out.

"Whoa. I'll take that." I hang it from the mirror. "There. It's great for our fake date. Plus"—I inhale through my nose—"it smells good."

"Fine."

"Seems like Charlotte could give your mema some competition as the romance expert."

"Which reminds me. Watch out for mistletoe when we arrive."

"Noted."

We fall into an easy conversation. Audrey tells me about her family's holiday traditions, decorating cookies for Santa, the Carlton Landing holiday home tour, and how competitive her cousins get during the Yuletide Challenge. I relax, almost forgetting we're driving toward a weekend of deception.

She taps the steering wheel. "Have we forgotten anything? What else do we need to know about each other?"

"I don't know. We've covered all the basics, right?"

"Oh, I know. What's your favorite color?"

"Wow. What a hard-hitting question."

"Hey, you never know."

"No one will ask you what my favorite color is."

"Answer the question, Harrison."

"Fine. Green."

"Light green or dark green?"

"Dark, like…I don't know, like something that's dark green."

"Like"—she glances around the car, then taps the little bundle, sending it swinging—"mistletoe?"

"No, not mistletoe. Something tough like hiking in a piney forest."

She giggles, and I frown. "What's yours, Blackwell?"

"Blue. Or maybe purple. It's a tie."

Her phone dings with a text, and the notification tells her it's on her group text. She swipes it open and hands it to me. "Can you tell me what this says?"

"Sure." I open the text thread and read. "'This is your final photo challenge! Let's take a walk down memory lane. Find a favorite Carlton Landing spot that brings back a memory or means something to you.'" I shrug. "This one's on you. I don't have any Carlton Landing memories."

"Oh, I know! Let's stop at the overlook. It's the first thing we'll pass before driving down into town."

"What memories do you have there?"

"Lots. Emma and I used to take picnics up there. We even did a sunrise breakfast once. Got up super early. But the real reason I want to use it is because it will be the memory of the first time I brought you."

Does she mean me or the Greyson version of me?

Either way, the corners of my mouth tilt up. "And it will be my first time here, so it will be memorable for me too."

"Exactly."

Her phone buzzes in my hand. "The first photo came through. It's of a couple posing in front of a chapel. It says 'where we got married.'" I recognize them from the snowman photo last night. Maybe I should study names while I'm not driving. One less thing to remember.

"Yeah. That's Hudson and Ava."

Another comes through. It's of two people lounging on a covered porch in a love seat. "One of your sisters?"

"Emma. And her boyfriend, Bryson. She's the one I was talking to that first day in the computer lab."

I nod. "It says, 'Lots of memories with Bryson out here. The first was years ago when I realized his family owned the house next door.'"

She giggles. "Ah. Their story was a long time in the making."

More photos trickle in over the next hour—including one with her aunt and uncle at some pizza place holding the remaining OREO truffles. And we work on our backstory, learn as much as possible about each other, and practice using my new name.

"Hey, Greyson," Audrey says. "I got another text. Will you check it?"

I smirk at her use of Greyson's name. This will take some getting used to. "Sure."

Someone sent a photo of a couple sitting on the dock, across the water, and far from the camera. They're side by side with their feet dangling over the edge. I try to zoom, but it's grainy.

"Can you tell who that is?" I show Audrey the phone, and she stiffens. Her brows pull together as she directs her gaze back out the front windshield.

"Is that a yes?"

She shakes out her shoulders. "Yeah, it's Drew. And his girlfriend. I don't know her name."

"Wait. Drew? As in the old crush?"

"That's the one."

Oh. "He's in Carlton Landing right now?"

"Yep. They live next door to Mema—the opposite side from Bryson's family—so she asked him and his parents to join in the Yuletide Challenge."

"Oh, I thought it was a family thing."

Her knuckles whiten on the steering wheel. "So did I."

I study her, but she doesn't turn my way. Something about this photo upsets her.

Her lips curve into a not-so-reassuring smile. "I only found out yesterday that he was participating."

Huh. The day she changed her mind about the double fake date and came running to me. Literally.

So far, in my head, this guy was a long-ago crush. A blast from the past. Some out-of-reach guy from years ago. But I'm getting the feeling her infatuation with him was much more recent.

I shift in my seat. "So they'll be around all weekend?"

"That's what I hear." Her voice dips. "They're also joining us for dinner tonight and most of the activities."

I nod, watching her profile. "Sounds like you've known him a long time."

"Seems like forever." She smiles, softer now, far away. "I had a crush on him from the moment we started going to Carlton Landing when I was thirteen."

Unease stirs in my stomach before I tamp it down.

Who is this guy? I won't ask more. That'd be pathetic. I'm not some jealous boyfriend.

I'm the *fake* boyfriend. I don't care.

I shouldn't care.

I keep my mouth shut, but…why exactly am I here?

17

Audrey

The Oklahoma landscape, farmland, forests, small towns, and truck stops, blur past the window. I steal glances at Jax. He's grown quiet, but I need him to talk so my mind will stop returning to our impromptu kiss. Did that happen? And how could I forget to take the photo? *Come on, Audrey.*

But...it didn't feel as fake as it should have.

Don't start thinking about it again.

But when I push the kiss from my mind, another image pops into my head. Drew and Miss Perfect posing on the dock with their feet resting on a floating paddleboard. That's how Drew and I spent our evenings last summer. He was busy flirting while I was busy falling even harder. Until his friends arrived and he no longer needed me to fill the time.

We were supposed to send a photo that brought back special memories. So why did he send *that* photo? He didn't send a kissing photo at all. What's he trying to say? That's *our* spot.

I shake the thoughts away. "So what else do we need to talk about for the weekend? Besides remembering to use your new name?"

Jax shifts, thoughtful. "We should discuss what they already know about Grey and go from there."

"I've been thinking about that, and thank goodness, it's not much. They know he's a sophomore biology major from Fort Worth and we have Organic Chemistry lab together. We became lab partners about halfway through the semester."

"I hope they don't ask me anything about that. I barely made it through Chem 1."

"Nah. They won't. They wouldn't know what to ask."

"Okay. Anything else?"

I crane, peering around a truck ahead. "I mentioned his birthday once. It's June eighteenth, and he turned twenty last summer. Oh, and we play pickleball together."

"Okay, yeah. I've played with him too."

I smirk. "Oh, good. So you won't look like a newbie on the Carlton Landing courts?"

He smirks back. "I'm at least as good as he is. Anyway, have you met his parents?"

"No. Have you?"

"Once at the beginning of the semester. But that doesn't matter if you haven't."

I tap my fingers to the upbeat Christmas song belting from my speakers as I remind him I have two sisters, each arriving with a boyfriend. "Lucy's in high school, and she and Connor have been together for over a year. And Emma started dating Bryson two months ago, so this is also his first Yuletide Challenge."

He rubs his palms on his jeans. "Got it. I met your mom. What's your dad like?"

"Quiet compared to Mom. But he's a softie. Poor guy had only girls."

We continue like this, asking questions, listening to music, and getting our story straight. We stop for gas in Eufaula, and I tell him all about when Morgan and Will met, an event involving an ICEE, gross gas-station coffee, and some major misunderstandings.

We get back on the road, and before we know it, we're turning off Highway 9 and through the stately Carlton Landing entrance. We wind along a narrow tree-lined road at a steady incline until we crest the hill. I park at the lookout. Even in the winter, four Adirondack chairs sit in a grassy area at the cliff's edge overlooking Lake Eufaula.

"Oh, wow." He opens his door and steps out onto the grass. "We can see for miles."

"Yep. And see that?" I nod to where pointed roofs peek from the trees near the water. With the sun low, Christmas lights already twinkle. "That's Carlton Landing."

He hooks his thumbs in his pockets and gazes into the distance. A chilly breeze rustles his hair. A smile tugs at his lips.

The same soft lips were against mine hours ago.

Nope, not thinking about that.

Instead, I pull my phone from my pocket and snap his photo as he stands on the edge of the world.

He turns, catching me, and his eyes gleam. "My first memory of Carlton Landing. Ready for that selfie?"

I move beside him and suck in a breath when he slides a hand around my waist. What is wrong with me? He either doesn't notice or pretends not to, so I extend my arm and take a photo with the cheery rooftops visible behind us.

I send it on the group text, and we head back to the car. Then I guide us down the hill to town and over a stone bridge. "This is it. Welcome to Carlton Landing."

He peers out the window, a grin stretching over his face. "You weren't kidding. This is straight out of a Christmas movie."

Each home has a distinct character while somehow maintaining a cohesive charm. Garlands hang from porches, wreaths adorn every door, and lights form stately rows along the rooflines and porch rails. A bundled family strolls down the sidewalk, enjoying the dying sunlight.

I take the long way and swing by the beach on Water Street.

"What's that?" He powers down his window as we pass a giant, two-story, cone-shaped Christmas tree made from leftover construction planks.

"Oh, that. You'll see. It was built earlier in the week for tomorrow night. A community tradition."

"Intriguing."

"Indeed." I veer onto a side street and stop in front of Mema's stately, two-story house. Warm light spills from every window, and laughter rumbles inside. I cut the engine. Nervous energy buzzes through my veins. "Last chance to back out."

I'm not sure which of us I'm talking to. Doesn't matter. The front door bursts open, and many of my family members spill out onto the wide front porch.

Jax lets out a nervous laugh. "Oh, we're committed."

"Looks like it." I rest a hand on his shoulder. "Thanks for doing this. Really." I lean over and kiss him on the cheek, and when I scoot back, he fixes me with his gray-blue gaze. A question sits between us, but I'm not sure what it is.

I wink to ease the tension. "For the onlookers… Greyson."

"Right." He faces the porch where my family waits.

We slip from the car and grab our bags. My family erupts with chatter and hugs. Christmas music pours from the open door, and decorations and lights brighten the porch.

I take Jax's hand and introduce him as Grey. Mom beams, Dad shakes his hand, polite but wary, and Lucy hugs him. I herd us inside to meet aunts, uncles, and cousins in a happy flurry of questions: Where did you meet? How long have you been dating?

When we reach the kitchen, which smells like the apple cider boiling on the stove, I lift a hand at the island. "Okay, okay. Calm down, everyone. This is Greyson, and we met in chemistry lab. We've been dating for what?"—I lower my hand to his shoulder—"a few months now?"

He nods. "Yeah, since September. It's nice to meet you all."

They launch into more questions. So far, they're ones we've gone over.

Luckily, my cousin's wife, Ava, steps in. "Let him breathe, people. You guys know you're overwhelming. I should know." She shoos them away good-naturedly.

I squeeze her hand and mouth, "Thank you."

Movement shifts in the doorway, and I swing my gaze in its direction. "Emma! Bryson!" I rush to them for hugs and then haul them to the island to meet Jax—er, Greyson.

"Guys, this is Grey. Grey, this is my sister Emma and her boyfriend, Bryson."

Emma's eyes are narrowed. She shakes his hand. "Nice to meet you. And welcome to our little slice of crazy."

She opens her mouth like she's about to ask something else, but a small hand reaches out to tug at Jax's sleeve.

Sophia, my ten-year-old cousin, tugs again. "Are you Audrey's boyfriend?"

"Yes. I'm Greyson. What's your name?"

"Sophia. And I like to make bracelets. I'll make you one too. What's your favorite color?"

His gaze snaps to mine, and I conjure my best I-told-you-so expression.

He rolls his eyes. "Dark green, I guess."

"Like mistletoe," I whisper, ruffling her hair.

"Oooh. Like Christmas magic. I'll add some red too."

Jax flaps his jaw. "Uh. Sure."

She points at me. "What's her favorite color?"

"Audrey likes blue and purple."

Sophia runs off, and Mema appears in the doorway, her silver hair styled elegantly, and the smile everyone says resembles mine in place.

"Mema!" I rush over and wrap her in a hug. I breathe in her familiar December-only peppermint scent. During the holidays, she dives headfirst into all things Christmassy, including perfume, hand soap, shampoo, everything.

"Hey, sweetie. I'm so glad you're here." She reaches for Jax. "And this must be the young man I've been hearing about. Greyson, I'm glad everything worked out for you to join us."

Her sharp gaze gives him a once-over before she pulls him into a hug. "I'm Wanda Davis, but most everyone else around here calls me Mema."

"It's nice to meet you, Mrs. Davis. Audrey talks about you all the time."

"All good things, I hope." She squeezes my shoulder. "I told you it would work out. Carlton Landing has a way of bringing people together. It's the place for romance and Christmas magic."

Oh boy. Here we go. My cheeks warm. "Mema, please don't start with that again." Especially with last night's kiss still fresh on my mind.

She pats Jax's arm. "You'll see. By the end of the weekend, you'll believe in the magic too."

Jax glances sidelong in my direction. "I certainly hope so."

The heat in my cheeks deepens. Super.

Mema waves overhead and waggles her eyebrows. "Keep a lookout for mistletoe opportunities."

Jax and I gaze out over the open living space, taking in its high ceilings.

You've got to be kidding.

His brows crimp together. "This place is a mistletoe land mine."

He's not wrong. At least six bunches booby-trap this room alone, most hanging above doorjambs and archways.

Mema giggles. "You're welcome."

I thread my fingers through Jax's. "It's something to watch out for. Don't pause in the doorways. Check."

He winks. "We'll see."

Uh-oh. Now, he's done it. He has Mema and her Christmas magic wrapped around his little finger.

She giggles again and then sighs. "My Harold would've loved this room and its kissing land mine."

I pat her shoulder with my free hand. "Without a doubt."

Mema recovers from her reverie, intent on showing Jax a photo of Papa, but her cell phone isn't in her pocket. "Oh, I must have left it upstairs when I took clean sheets up. Audrey, be a doll and run up to fetch it from the guest bedroom nightstand."

"Sure." I squeeze Jax's fingers. "You good?"

He nods and squeezes back. "I'm good."

I release his hand and bound up the stairs. As I round the corner into the room, the front door's creak echoes up the stairs, followed by the chattering of my family's collective greeting.

Oh no. There's only one family I haven't seen yet.

Aunt Suzanne's voice carries up the stairs. "The Edwards are here!"

I sink onto the bed and groan.

Drew, his parents, and Miss Perfect have arrived.

18

Jax

The front door closes, cutting off the cold, and Audrey's family moves to greet the newcomers, a couple about my parents' age, followed by a tall, good-looking guy and a beautiful blonde.

I don't recognize them right away.

Mrs. Davis waves over the crowd, and I lean her way. "Who are they?"

"Oh, those are our neighbors. The Edwards. That's their son, Drew, and that must be his girlfriend. I'd better go say hi."

As she shuffles into the living room, my eyebrows shoot high on my forehead. *That's* Drew? Mr. Six Foot

Three with a perfect haircut and a perfect tan who obviously works out is Audrey's longtime crush?

This is who she's been in love with since she was thirteen?

That's just great.

Alone, I step back into the shadows, not quite ready to be pulled into the fray to meet anyone new. Especially him.

Movement above catches my eye as Audrey emerges like a Christmas angel at the top of the stairs. No one else looks up in all the commotion. She's… beautiful.

Pausing, she watches Drew. Her fingers grip the handrail. She smooths out her hair and starts her descent.

Before I can scrutinize her reaction, Lucy bounds up the stairs and pushes Audrey back up and out of sight.

Pressure on my elbow has me turning. Emma has snuck up behind me.

"Hey—*you*." She says it like she's forgotten my name. She has my bag, which I dropped by the front door. "Let me show you to your room upstairs. Audrey and Lucy are already up there."

"Um, okay." I take the bag, and we trudge up the stairs, avoiding Drew and his family.

At the landing, she knocks on a door, and it opens to reveal Lucy. Her hand reaches out, grabs my arm, and yanks me into the room. Emma pushes from behind.

"Hey." I spin around. I'm standing next to Audrey, her mouth also slanted into a confused frown.

"What are you guys doing?" Audrey crosses her arms. "What's going on?"

Emma shuts and locks the door. She mimics Audrey and crosses her arms, shifting her weight onto one foot.

Am I being kidnapped? *What* did I walk into?

"Okay, *Greyson*." Emma says Grey's name like it's a curse and glares in my direction. "Who are you?"

19

Audrey

My mouth drops open, and I gape at Emma, arms crossed and eyes narrowed. Lucy hovers behind her, shuffling from foot to foot.

How did they figure it out so quickly? We've been here, what, twenty minutes?

Our perfect double fake date is going up in smoke like the logs in the fireplace.

Jax's wide-eyed gaze meets mine. He says nothing, leaving the response up to me.

That's fair.

What do we do? Deny it? Maybe they don't know that much. I uncross my arms and put on my best confused face. "What are you talking about?"

"I know he's not Greyson."

Tread carefully. "What exactly do you think you know?"

Emma rolls her eyes and slips her phone from her pocket. She swipes the screen and then tips it to me. "This is Greyson."

It's Grey's Instagram account. And there's his photo. Grey posts all the time, but not usually of people. He's more into esthetic shots. Emma must have scrolled to find this one. But we never took any photos together. And besides, I checked his account to be sure. "That doesn't tell me much."

She scrolls for several seconds and then extends the screen to us again. "And there's you. The caption says. 'Killed it in Chem lab today.'"

It's a selfie of Greyson in his white coat and goggles. I'm at our table in the background, facing the front of the room, my goggles already off.

She lifts a palm. "I looked him up after you mentioned him over fall break. You said he was your chemistry partner."

My face warms. I never saw that post. I didn't even know he took the photo. He must have done it before we started dating. Ironic, really.

Emma waves the phone around. "He wasn't hard to find, and here you are, Greyson's chemistry partner.

So…" She displays the photo again. "I was expecting to see this guy." She jabs her thumb in Jax's general direction. "Not Mr. Tall, Dark-Haired, and Dimples."

My shoulders sag. "Okay, fine. Yes, that's my ex-boyfriend, my chem lab partner, Greyson."

Lucy tilts her head toward Jax. "So who is he?"

Jax meets my gaze, his gray-blue eyes asking a silent question. I nod, permitting him to drop the act.

"I'm Jaxton. Greyson's roommate."

I sink onto Emma's daybed, exhausted. "I've known Jax as long as I've known Grey." I lift a shoulder. "After Grey dumped me *last week*, I was content to hide forever and even skip Christmas. Then Jax came to the tutoring lab to study for his final. He talked me through it, and we came up with this idea. Which, admittedly, is turning out to be a bad one."

Emma rounds on Jax, stabbing a finger in his direction. "You. Why would you go along with this?"

A sheepish grin. "It was mutually beneficial?"

"What?"

"It was a double fake date. Last night, she pretended to be my girlfriend at a wedding I didn't want to go to. She even stood up to my ex-girlfriend." He sends me a wink. "It was brilliant."

Lucy's gaze flips between us like she's watching a pickleball match. Something like surprise or suspicion arches her features. She joins me on the bed and tucks her legs under her. "Why didn't you tell us about Greyson?"

"I was planning on it. Then Mema couple-ified the Yuletide Challenge, and everyone was so excited to finally meet Grey, and…then…" No way am I bringing up Drew's name.

Emma stares at me like I've grown a second head. "Do you realize how crazy this is? You're the big sister. The responsible one. The perfect child. What happens when everyone finds out you've been lying?"

Jax moves to Emma's desk chair and sinks into it, leaning forward to put his elbows on his knees. "Our plan was to break up after the holidays."

"And then I'd tell the truth," I add. "Once enough time had passed. It's not that big a deal."

"Not a big deal?" Emma's voice rises. "Audrey, this is *our* family we're talking about. This is Mema, who lives for this holiday stuff and believes in the magic and romance of Carlton Landing. Who put up twelve— twelve!—mistletoe bunches around the house. What happens when she finds out your romance is fake? And what will Mom say? And you, sir, should worry about what Dad will *do*." She points at Jax and then jabs at me. "And how much more will all the cousins give you a hard time after this?"

Emma's gaze drifts into the distance. "That's it. That's what this is about. It's because Drew is here."

"No! It's not."

She cocks her head to the side. "Aud."

"It's not completely about that."

Jax's jaw is tight, and his hands hold his sudden interest. What does he make of this?

I plunge on. "It's everything. It's about not wanting to be the only single person during a couples' challenge. It's about not wanting to disappoint Mom…or Mema." Tears prick my eyes. "About not wanting to explain to everyone that my boyfriend dumped me days before Christmas break."

Lucy rubs circles on my back. "Let it go, Emma."

She's uncharacteristically stern, which must be why Emma breathes out a sigh and lets her arms drop to her sides.

"This is crazy," she says.

"I know it's not ideal." I straighten and push my hair over my shoulder. "But we're here now. What do you want me to do? Go downstairs and come clean?"

Emma opens her mouth, then closes it. She knows there's no good answer.

And what would that mean for Jax?

He meets my gaze. "I shouldn't stay if you do that. I could get an Uber home."

"That would cost hundreds of dollars. If you could even find a driver at all from out here. And then you'd be home alone until your parents get out of the mountains."

He shrugs.

"That would ruin Christmas for everyone." Lucy stands and paces. "Especially Mema. Bring in unnecessary drama."

"Yeah, maybe." Emma kneads her temples. "But that would make us part of her lie."

I stand. "It's just for the rest of the weekend. Then I'll take Jax back to the city where we'll have an amicable breakup…when it won't ruin Christmas."

Hands on hips, Emma accosts Jax. "What do you think?"

"I'm in if you are."

"You guys have to sell it."

Jax's dimple folds into his cheek. "We've been practicing."

Lucy grins. Thank goodness, someone knocks on the door before she can say whatever is on her mind.

Emma's boyfriend, Bryson, edges the door inward. He pitches his voice low. "Did you find out who the impostor is?" Great. He's smiling like this is the most exciting thing he's ever been a part of.

I roll my eyes. "He knows too? Who else?"

Emma loops an arm through Bryson's. "Lucy, did you tell your moody boyfriend?"

"No. And I don't think I will. He's acting weird."

"Then it's the five of us."

"Okay, then." I exhale. Some of the weight leaves my chest.

"Come on." Bryson beckons Jax. "I'll show you the loft. That's where you and the moody boyfriend will sleep."

Jax stands. "Where will you be?"

Bryson motions out the window. "Oh, I live next door. I'll be there."

"Right." Jax takes a deep breath. He squeezes my hand as he passes, and I give him a weary, here-we-go kind of grimace. "I'll meet you downstairs in a few minutes."

Lucy smirks.

Bryson whispers something like, "Uh, so what's your name?" as they step out onto the landing.

Lucy closes the door and leans against it, and I'm barricaded in with the girls.

Emma sags into the desk chair. "Seriously, Audrey. Why didn't you tell us Greyson broke up with you? We could have convinced Mema to change the rules of the Challenge."

I flop down on the bed again and cover my face with a pillow. "I don't know." The pillow muffles my groan. "I was embarrassed."

Lucy snatches the pillow into her lap after joining me on the mattress again. "What happened? With the breakup, I mean?"

Out comes a brief recap of all that happened, to which they are appropriately irate. Then I go into Mom calling at the Lighting of the Commons, and Emma telling me Drew was participating, and my race to catch Jax before he left.

"Wow." Lucy giggles. "You've had an interesting few days."

Emma picks at her holiday-themed nail polish. "So Drew was the final straw?"

"Yeah, I guess."

"Does this have anything to do with last summer?"

I twist my hands together, and my fingertips go reddish purple. "Maybe. You already know Drew flirted with me off and on through the years. He knew I liked him, and he liked the attention. But last summer, when we were here for the Fourth of July, it was different. He sought me out. He showered me with attention. He kept saying how different I looked, how I'd grown up. We stayed up talking by the lake until midnight. Nothing happened between us, but I felt the potential was there… and my dreams were coming true."

"How did I not know about this?" Lucy scrunches her eyebrows.

"Probably because I didn't tell you. And I was glad I didn't because the next day, two families who rent over by Redbud Park arrived with some of his older friends. Suddenly, he had options. He went back to treating me like his kid sister and acting as if nothing ever happened between us. Which, I guess, it hadn't. I was a convenient distraction when no one else was around."

"So you wanted to make him jealous?"

"Not exactly. I wanted him to know I'd moved on. I wanted him to know he can't keep drawing me in and playing with my emotions." I grab the green pendant against my chest and slide it down its chain. "I'm sorry I got you guys involved. I see now it was idiotic."

"It's okay." Lucy loops an arm around me. "That's pretty."

I turn the pendant in my fingers. "It has an interesting story. Jax bought it for me…sort of."

"Jax, the fake boyfriend, bought you a necklace?"

"Yeah." I tell them the story.

By the end, Lucy is smirking again.

I tuck the necklace back in my sweater. "What?"

"Nothing."

Emma, who'd been pacing again, whips around to face me, her eyes wide. She points at the door where the boys disappeared. "Wait. Audrey Dianne Blackwell, you kissed that boy for the Challenge. On the lips."

My cheeks warm. "Uh, yeah."

The memory flashes through my mind, Jax's arm around my waist, my hand on his chest—nope, don't go there.

"It was nothing. It wasn't real, and it didn't mean anything."

Emma's expression says she doesn't believe me. "Well, I hope you know what you're doing. I certainly don't."

Lucy flips through her phone. "You have to admit, though. He's dreamy. Way cuter than that photo of Greyson." She holds out the phone as she waggles her eyebrows. "And check out that kiss. It looks real to me."

"Lucy! Put that away." I try to sound stern as I swat at her hand, but I can't squelch an intrusive smile. Even Emma is smiling now.

"What? It's true." Lucy holds her phone out of reach.

"Calm down. It's all fake. And don't forget he's my ex-boyfriend's roommate."

"Lucy, don't encourage a romance with the fake date!" Emma tosses a pillow at her, only to have it tossed right back. "How would Audrey know what's real and what isn't if they're pretending all the time?" She launches the pillow at me. "And *you* need to stay laser-focused so no one figures this out. I don't want anyone to know I got dragged into it."

"You're right. Of course, you're right. I'm focused." I'm the responsible one. I would never fall for my fake date, even if I were dumb enough to bring one.

And how *would* I know if anything was real?

I wouldn't.

I stand and smooth my sweater. "Let's focus by going downstairs before Mema sends a search party."

They're still giggling as they follow me onto the landing, where another bunch of mistletoe hangs overhead.

Land mine, indeed.

All this romantic vegetation brings that great kiss to mind. The twinkling Christmas lights of the town square, the softness of Jax's lips against mine, the unexpected sparks. It didn't feel like nothing.

But it was.

Everything is an act, including the kiss. It didn't mean anything to me, and it didn't mean anything to him.

Though the kiss was fantastic, and no matter how nice he is or how cute Lucy thinks he is—and he *is* cute—this is all temporary. A Christmas charade that will end by Monday.

And since I don't need any more kisses with Jaxton Harrison to muddle our already confused double-fake-date plan, I steer clear of the mistletoe.

20

Audrey

The stairs creak beneath our feet as my sisters and I descend into the disorder that is our family Christmas dinner. I graze my fingers along the wooden banister, avoiding the garland wrapped around it, so I don't ski down the stairs in my fuzzy holiday socks.

First things first. I don't want to sit anywhere near Drew, so I locate him. His elbow is propped on the mantel as he talks to his gorgeous date. My stomach does an uncomfortable flip, but I force my gaze away before he notices. When I locate Jax, already with Bryson in the dining room, I find his gaze fixed on me, his handsome face unreadable.

He was watching me watch Drew.

Super.

Farmhouse Christmas decorations clutter every surface. Red and green twinkling lights reflect off rustic gold ornaments. Fresh pine garlands drape across the mantel and wind up the stair railing, lending their crisp scent. Furniture has been pushed against the walls and into corners to make room for folding tables draped in red snowflake-patterned tablecloths. The dining room table has been extended with card tables at both ends.

My dad and some other adults arrange folding chairs around the tables. Others tend the food and plate it for the little ones. And in the center of it all, Mema directs the chaos like a holiday orchestra conductor, her enormous wreath earrings glinting in the light as she points and instructs.

"Girls," she calls when we descend the stairs. "You'll be on dish duty tonight along with Hudson and Will."

I give her a thumbs-up and weave through the maze until I'm standing next to Jax. His lips lift into a warm smile that's probably all for show.

I lean close. "You good…Grey?"

"Yeah, I'm good."

Mema taps a fork against a glass, and the room quiets. "Before we dig in, I want to say how blessed I feel to have so many of you here this Christmas. Thank you for taking the time. I wish Harold were here to see this full house. He would've loved it."

Murmurs of assent respond, and then Jax threads his fingers through mine as Uncle Clint prays over our meal.

Dinner is served buffet style, so we make our way through, loading our plates with all the usual holiday comfort foods: spiral-sliced ham, turkey, green-bean casserole, sweet potatoes topped with marshmallows, and, of course, Mema's famous homemade yeast rolls.

She stacks an extra roll on Jax's plate as we pass. "Here, sweetie. You'll want two."

My family's chaotic energy enlivens the space as everyone finds a seat, and the little ones are ushered onto the back porch for a picnic under the heat lamps. Christmas music plays beneath the din of conversation.

I guide Jax to the living room, where my parents have already settled at a long table with Uncle Bob and Aunt Suzanne. They're deep in conversation about the upcoming bonfire.

Jax pulls out a chair for me at the other end. "Your grandma's cool."

"She is. She's also watching our every move." I shake my head, settling into my seat. "She's probably trying to catch us under the mistletoe."

Once seated, Jax glances over his shoulder and gives a slight wave to Mema, who doesn't even pretend she wasn't staring. She beams and waves back.

"Smooth." I giggle.

"Will all these people stay the night?"

"No way. There's barely enough seating, much less beds. My family and our guests will stay here, as my dad technically owns the house. Everyone else will stay in local rental properties."

Lucy and Emma slide into seats across from us, followed by their boyfriends. Lucy gifts me an encouraging grin while Emma narrows her eyes at Jax like he's the key suspect in an identity-theft case. Which, I suppose, he is.

"So, Greyson," my dad begins, "Audrey tells us you two study chemistry together?"

"Yes, sir." Jax's voice is steady, without a trace of awkwardness. "Actually, your daughter has saved my grade more than once."

Mom nods. "She's always had a knack for science. Gets that from her father." She stabs a green bean onto her fork. "I know you're from Texas, but do you have any family in Oklahoma?"

Jax answers their questions with ease.

I listen, searching for cracks in his story, but so far, so good. I chance a glance across the room and regret it when I lock eyes with Drew.

He raises an eyebrow, a half smile on his lips.

My heart does a little flutter, a remnant of all the disappointed hopes over the years. I refocus on my plate and tear off a piece of my roll.

Ten minutes later, after Mema has made sure everyone is served, she joins our table and asks Jax the same questions all over again. He doesn't miss a beat.

Then, of course, she turns the conversation to Carlton Landing romance.

"Is that how you and your husband met?" Jax asks.

Emma pats Mema's hand. "She and Grandpa were the original lakeside romance."

Jax sets his fork down. "Really? Do tell."

"Oh, now you've done it." Mom's eyes gleam, her smile fond.

"Oh, hush, Linda." Mema swats at the air. "These young people need to know how it's done."

She settles back in her chair. "Our story, of course, didn't happen at Carlton Landing because the town didn't exist back then, but it *was* on the lake, closer to Eufaula. We met at the end of June when we were both visiting for some fun in the sun. I was twenty, and he was twenty-two. He was down from OKC with friends for the weekend, and I was with extended family for a weeklong vacation. I arrived on a Saturday and met Harold that evening."

Several family members, including the children who've returned from their picnic in search of seconds, have paused to listen, though we've all heard it before.

Mema's eyes gleam like she's transported back in time. "I'd been out on the boat with my cousins, and I wanted to come back to shore because I was feeling motion sick. I thought we would all go in, but no, they dropped me off on the dock and took off again. And guess who came running up the bridge at that moment?"

My ten-year-old cousin Sophia raises her hand like she's at school, waving her dinner roll overhead. "Papa!"

"That's right, sweetie!" Mema takes a sip of her sweet tea. "His friends played a joke on him by leaving to go out on the boat while Harold was taking a nap. So there we were, the two of us side by side, watching our friends sail away into the evening without us. It was the best thing that ever happened to me."

Brooklyn, my twelve-year-old cousin, sighs dreamily, and Emma whispers under her breath. "Such a fabulous meet-cute."

I raise an eyebrow at my romance novel-loving sister.

She shrugs. "It is."

Mema adjusts her wedding ring, the tiny diamond glittering. "So we started talking, and when Harold's friends came back to get him, he waved them off and stayed to chat instead. I learned he was from Edmond, like my aunt and uncle, and he liked red velvet cake and country music and was studying to be an engineer. I shared my favorite song and told him I loved going to the movies and hoped to become a teacher when I finished university. We talked about everything and nothing. We spent a lot of time together the next day. We went to the local diner, and he played my favorite song on the jukebox. We competed in the community Olympics and even won first place in the three-legged race. But then, as all good things do, the weekend came to an end, and Harold left. I'd planned on plucking up the courage to ask if he wanted my number, but he left before I could. I worried I'd never see him again."

Jax wipes his mouth with a napkin. "But you did. What happened?"

"Well, since he never asked for any information that would allow him to contact me again, I wasn't sure he liked me that way." She lifts her hands. "But sometimes, a girl has to make her own opportunities, you know? How would I ever know for sure if I didn't try? So, I called my aunt, who lives in Edmond, and she helped me locate his address in the city directory. Hang on. I'll show you what I sent."

Mema pushes back her chair and rushes off to her bedroom. Back in a flash, she holds an old, worn envelope. "I wanted to be subtle. Hint that I wanted him to come back without putting too much pressure on him."

She removes a faded blue ribbon and an old photograph. "I sent our first-place ribbon for the three-legged race and this photograph." It's of them holding out their ribbon. "This is our first-ever photo taken together. Listen to what I wrote on the back: 'It was a good day. I knew from the second I saw you that you were someone I could like. But then you disappeared.'"

She slips a sheet of creamy stationery from the envelope. "And I wrote him this letter, hinting at exactly where I would be on the Fourth of July, even going so far as to say I thought he'd enjoy the fireworks and red velvet cake."

Jax chuckles. "So, he got the hint?"

"Oh yes. He showed up just in time for the festivities. He surprised me with flowers and declarations of love. He even had the live band play my song. We watched fireworks together on the beach, and this time, before he left, he got my number. It turns out he came to find me before he left, but we were out to dinner at the time. His friends wouldn't wait. He thought that was it."

Mom pats her on the arm. "He was a keeper."

Uncle Bob wags his eyebrows. "The original ladies' man."

Everyone laughs, and Mema leans our way. "Well, after that day, he was a one-woman man, but yes, it was very romantic."

Jax settles back in his chair. "That's a great story, Mrs. Davis."

"Yes, it is. So you see, this lake is magical. Not literal magic, of course. But more like…magical opportunities. Opportunities that could change the course of your life."

She winks at me, and I nearly choke on my water.

She raises her glass. "To family, to love, and to finding some Christmas magic!"

"Hear, hear," Mom says, and those of us at our table raise our glasses and then chink them together.

The people in the dining room crane their necks to see what we're up to. I lock eyes with Drew again and dart my gaze away.

As dinner progresses, Jax fits in with my family. He asks my dad about his work-from-home engineering job. He commiserates with my mom, a high school English teacher, about end-of-semester grading. And he even manages to get a smile out of Emma when he tells her he plans to buy a copy of her self-published book. No way the real Greyson could've done this well with my family.

Jax is so different from my impression over the semester. He was solemn and standoffish whenever Grey and I were around him. I thought he didn't like me, or, at least, he was overly quiet and focused. But here, surrounded by my family, he's attentive, charming, and surprisingly funny.

He listens closely as Lucy's boyfriend, Connor, talks about his college plans. I haven't *really* looked at Jax since the kiss, opting on our drive to stare out the windshield and avoid his gaze. Now, while he talks, his dark hair falls across his forehead, and the slight dimple appears when he smiles. He nods along when Connor drones on, like he sometimes does.

"You're staring," Lucy whispers in my ear as she reaches across me for the salt.

I blink. "No, I'm not."

The others are intent on what Mom is jabbering on about, so Lucy stays close. She grins and shakes salt onto her mashed potatoes. "Yes, you are. Is it possible my big sis *likes* her fake boyfriend?"

"Shh. Don't talk about that here. Besides, you're supposed to think I like him. That's the point."

Lucy smirks and returns to her meal.

With dessert underway, Mema announces that the next Yuletide Challenge, a puzzle-solving contest, will commence after the plates are cleared and the tables are rearranged.

Groans and cheers erupt.

I push back from the table. "I need coffee for this. Anyone else want some?"

Hands go up, and I take orders before heading to the kitchen. I'm filling the coffee maker with water when footsteps shuffle behind me.

"Were you ever going to say hi to me?"

I freeze, because I'd recognize that voice anywhere. Drew Edwards.

He slides in next to me and braces a hip against the counter with the effortless confidence that always made me weak in the knees. His light-brown hair is shorter this time, but those hazel eyes are the same—intense, amused, demanding attention.

I turn back to the machine and measure ground coffee into the filter. "Hey, Drew." It comes out quieter than I intended. "How are you?"

"Good. Staying busy with PA school." He inches closer. "It's been a while."

"Yeah."

"Too long, maybe."

I glance his way before pushing the start button, but don't say anything.

"You look good, Aud. College life must be treating you well."

The familiar way he says my nickname sends an annoying flutter through my stomach, but I'm not sure it's butterflies. Probably more like mosquitoes. Lots of them. I tamp down the coffee grounds with more force than necessary. "It is. Sophomore year has been great."

"I was surprised you brought someone." His voice drops a notch. "You usually fly solo at these things."

Thanks for the reminder. I shrug. "A lot has changed this semester."

"I can see that."

He stoops to rest his elbows on the counter. "Sasha may not get to stay the whole time. Her family wants her to come to an event tomorrow."

"That's too bad." It's not.

"I was hoping you and I could team up for the Challenge tomorrow." His fingers brush against mine as he reaches for a mug. He retreats, gazing over my shoulder. Louder, he says, "But lucky for us, your boyfriend's schedule freed up."

I inch away as a hand rests on my lower back. Jax is there, his face inches from mine. But he's not looking at me.

21

Jax

"Lucky us." I circle my palm over Audrey's back. "I came to see if you need any help."

"That'd be great."

Drew straightens, making himself taller than me while creating more space, but not backing away. "You must be the boyfriend."

I extend a hand. "I'm Greyson."

He takes it, gripping tighter than necessary. "Drew. Family friend. Audrey and I go *way* back."

A muscle flexes in my jaw. The coffee maker starts dripping, and I slide my arm back around Audrey's waist. "So, I've heard."

And though his girlfriend is in the next room, his gaze lingers on Audrey in the same way Greyson's used to follow other girls when she wasn't around. I dislike him instantly.

Perhaps she's thinking this same thing because she leans into me. "We haven't had a chance to meet your girlfriend. How'd you two meet?"

He smiles like he sees what she's doing, but plays along. "Sasha and I have mutual friends. They introduced us." He points between us. "What about you guys?"

Audrey nudges me with her shoulder. "Grey's my lab partner at school."

Drew pulls a Christmassy coffee mug toward himself across the countertop. The sound grates. "Oh, yeah? For which class?"

"Organic Chemistry," I say.

He scrutinizes me. "Nice. I took that. Barely pulled the A, but I got it in the end."

Oh, great. He's a bragger.

And about to ask some technical questions I'm not qualified to answer.

But Audrey's quick to change the subject. "Drew's family owns the house next door. I've known him since we first started coming to Carlton Landing."

Drew hooks his thumbs in his belt loops. "Yep. The two of us practically grew up together. Lots of history, right, Aud?"

Before she can comment on their *history*, Mrs. Davis's voice carries from the next room. "Audrey! Is the coffee ready? We need to get the puzzle challenge going."

"Just a sec," Audrey calls. "I had to brew a new pot." She picks up a Grinch-themed mug and addresses Drew. "I'd better get this finished up. And you should get back. Your girlfriend will wonder where you are."

A flash of something—annoyance, maybe—tightens Drew's face.

He grabs the coffeepot and pours himself the first cup as his confident smile slides back into place. "Puzzle challenge. My specialty. Well, may the best team win." He salutes me with his mug. "Fair warning, though, I don't like to lose."

Something ignites in my chest. I've never been that competitive, but this guy makes me want to crush him at puzzling.

Words I never expected to cross my mind.

He saunters off, and I let my hand drop to my side. "That's your childhood crush? What a dirtball."

She chuckles, watching him out of the kitchen. "He's not usually like that. Something must be bothering him. I figured he'd be all happy, gloating about his beautiful girlfriend and all."

"First of all, *my* girlfriend is beautiful. That's you, by the way. Second…" I lean back to peer around the doorway and lower my voice. "The thing that is bothering him is that I'm here. You brought another guy, and he hates it."

She pours coffee into mugs, her cheeks pink. "That's ridiculous. He hardly ever gives me the time of day. He's in a mood."

As we join the others in the living room, both of us carrying multiple coffees, her gaze flicks to Drew.

Is this whole ruse more than helping her save face at Christmas dinner?

Am I here…to make him jealous?

My stomach sinks. She didn't mention it before, but if it is true, I don't have any reason to be disappointed. I'm not *actually* her jealous boyfriend.

But a competition I didn't know I was a part of is brewing.

And not just the yuletide thing.

I catch Drew's searing glare again.

I do not want him to win.

Once everyone has finished dessert and the tables have been cleared, we gather around the living room. Mrs. Davis stands in the center, a clipboard pressed to her chest, reading glasses perched on her nose. "Before we begin our puzzle race, I want to share the current standings after the photo challenge." She runs a pencil down her notes. "In the first place, we have Morgan and Will."

As a couple I recognize from introductions earlier high-fives across the room, a deep voice calls from behind me. "What? They cheated on one of the photos?"

Someone groans. Others cackle.

Mrs. Davis peers over her glasses at him. "Do not question the scorekeeper, Hudson."

She rattles off more figures until she gets to the bottom. "And tied for last place, mostly due to time and submission penalties"—she pauses for effect—"Audrey and Greyson and Drew and Sasha."

Super. We're tied with the childhood crush. For last place.

As everyone starts chattering, Drew and I make eye contact. He glowers.

Oh, it's on.

Mrs. Davis whistles with two fingers against her mouth. "Pipe down, everyone. Each team has the same never-before-opened, three-hundred-piece puzzle. Don't open it until I say go. First place will receive ten points, second place nine, third place eight, and so on. Sabotaging another team's puzzle is grounds for disqualification. Now, spread out and make sure you have enough room."

Once everyone is settled, the older adults claim the tables, and the rest of us find patches of floor. Mrs. Davis raises a hand. "Ready, set, go!"

The room erupts with boxes being upturned and puzzle pieces clattering onto tables.

Audrey starts flipping all ours right side up. "Border pieces first?"

"Definitely." I grab the box lid to study the image. A vintage Christmas scene—a small town covered in snow.

Without further discussion, we fall into a rhythm, sorting pieces and connecting them in surprising efficiency. My fingers brush against hers as we pass pieces back and forth, and her cheeks flush. Must be the competitive energy, but it's cute anyway.

We continue, communicating in half sentences and nods while we identify patterns.

Huh. We're in sync for two people in a fabricated relationship.

"Done!" The voice comes from one of the adult tables. It's the lady who included the snowman container in all her photos. The rest of the participants groan good-naturedly.

Mrs. Davis claps. "Keep going, everyone! Who will take second?"

Another couple finishes before us.

Then Audrey slides a completed portion of the townscape toward me, and I connect it with the church steeple I've been working on. "Done!" we yell out as I fit the final piece. She laughs, a bright, infectious sound.

Mrs. Davis hurries over to inspect our work. "Nice job, you two. Third place!"

We high-five, and she giggles, planting a kiss on my cheek like we won the Super Bowl. My heart does a little flip as if I threw the winning touchdown.

Smiling, I sneak a glance at Drew. He's scowling down at their pile of remaining pieces, and his girlfriend's body language says the puzzling isn't going well.

A couple of other groups finish before he signals they're done.

Mrs. Davis updates her clipboard, putting us three points ahead of them.

Nice.

Next is the children's board-game tournament, where we play quick games of Hungry Hippos, Jenga, and Connect Four in bracket play. Audrey and I only won one of our three matches, but we don't have to play Drew, so that in itself is a *W*.

Through it all, we play our parts well, though…I am having fun. That part's not an act. I'm enjoying my time with this crazy family.

And catching Drew glaring in our direction is the icing on the cake.

Once we're out of the tournament, Audrey skips off to the kitchen for a coffee refill, leaving me sitting near Bryson on the living room rug.

He leans my way, nodding toward Drew. "I don't think he likes you."

"Yeah, I caught that. Weird that he's acting so jealous when his girlfriend is right there."

Bryson snorts. "They've been fighting all evening. And he's been telling everyone they're 'just talking' and not actually together. I wonder if she knew that before coming here." He lowers his voice. "Emma says Drew's always had a thing for Audrey, but only when it's convenient. Maybe he was counting on getting her attention all weekend." He claps me on the back and jostles me. "But then you showed up."

This information settles uncomfortably in my chest as the tournament turns to a deafening game of Hungry Hippos. The battle rages, and Sasha approaches Mrs. Davis and gives her a hug. "Thank you for everything, but I'm off to my next holiday event. Merry Christmas."

They exchange a warm goodbye, Mrs. Davis promises to partner with Drew for the rest of the Challenge, and then Drew walks Sasha out onto the front porch.

When he returns, alone, his gaze wanders straight to Audrey.

Super.

The match ends in groans and cheers, and something tells me this weekend is about to get even more complicated.

But as Mrs. Davis raps on her clipboard with a pen, Audrey makes her way to *me*. Joining me on the rug and sitting close, she tucks her shoulder slightly behind mine against the couch. Her fingers wrap around the Grinch mug as she shoots me a shy smile. I couldn't tame my answering smile if I wanted to.

Mrs. Davis reclaims everyone's attention. "Who's ready to set up for the annual gingerbread-making contest?" Cheers erupt, and she doles out instructions, sending some to set the younger kids up outside for their noncompetitive decorating while directing others to gather supplies. I'm assigned to a table-rearranging group.

Once everything is situated to her liking, Mrs. Davis gets things started. "Okay, for the gingerbread-house challenge, we're switching to larger teams. I've paired each couple with another couple."

Does she hate me enough to put us with Drew? But when she calls our names, she says, "Audrey and Grey will join Bryson and Emma. And Drew and I will team up with Lucy and Connor. Take five minutes to gather what you need from the kitchen, and remember, you can always go back and get more."

We get set up, and the competition begins.

Emma grabs one of the gingerbread-house-making kits. Bryson and I load up on gumdrops, gummy bears, and M&Ms. I raise an eyebrow when Audrey returns to our table with a hot glue gun. "Isn't that cheating?"

"Not in this house," Emma says. "We're allowed to use the glue gun to hold the walls and roof of the house together. We used to try to do it with icing, but everything falls apart and causes a lot of frustration. And in some cases"—she cuts her gaze to Lucy— "tears."

Audrey slides the plug into an outlet. "Be nice. She was like ten at the time."

"Way too old to cry about a gingerbread house." Emma shakes her head. "Baby of the family."

I open the package of glue sticks and point one at her. "Hey, I'm a youngest child."

"Shh." Audrey forces my hand down. "Yeah, but Grey's not."

I make a face. "Right."

Since Emma and Bryson know the truth about me, we speak in hushed tones about how it's all going while we smear white icing over our roof. Emma grills me with questions, intent on unearthing my life's story, which isn't that exciting.

I want to cheer when Bryson turns the conversation to Drew and his death glares. He asks the question I've been wanting answered. "What is up with that guy?"

Audrey shrugs and places a gumdrop along the roofline. "Who knows?"

Emma rolls her eyes and gives a real answer. "Drew's been hanging around since we were kids. But he's a player."

"Emma." Audrey nudges her sister.

Who ignores her. "He and Audrey had this *almost* thing last summer. Flirting, hanging out by the lake, and so on. But then his friends showed up, and he was too busy for her."

Audrey's cheeks have pinked. "It wasn't a *thing*. We were just friends."

"Uh-huh. That's why you spent two days moping in your room?"

"Well, he hurt my feelings. He ignored me the rest of the summer. Made me feel like an idiot."

Emma's hard look softens. "He's the idiot, not you. He never should have treated you like that, like you were too young or in the way all of a sudden. Whatever was between you, you deserve better."

That confirms it. Audrey's crush on Drew is not ancient history. In her mind, something was between them as little as six months ago. Maybe Drew is acting jealous simply because he is. Maybe he's changed his mind and ready to start something with her.

If that's why she brought me here and he's now free of his girlfriend, what does she want? Does she want to give it a chance since he seems interested?

And where does that leave me?

Should I tell her how I feel?

There were moments over the past week when I thought she might like me. But what if I'm wrong? What if she still likes him?

It's my ex-girlfriend all over again. At first, I wondered if Audrey would go back to Grey, just as Zoe had gone back to her ex while dating me. But it's not Grey I should've been worried about. If Audrey "goes back" to anyone, it will be Drew. And I'll be the rebound guy all over again.

We continue working, adding M&Ms around the windows. Across the room, Drew laughs with Mrs. Davis. Others around them join in.

He fits in so naturally. He's been around for so long, it's as if he's family.

And what about me? Who am I?

Just the guy lying to everyone.

22

Audrey

The next morning, the kitchen smells like vanilla and warm butter as I flip perfectly golden pancakes onto the growing stack. Outside Mema's kitchen window, the morning sun glitters across the lake, promising another beautiful winter day in Carlton Landing. I've always loved these quiet mornings before everyone else stumbles down, hair disheveled and eyes still sleep puffy. Just me and Mema, working in comfortable silence, the only sounds the sizzle of batter hitting the griddle and the melody of Christmas music coming from the living room speaker.

"Those look perfect, honey." Mema slides a bowl of fresh-cut strawberries onto the island. She's already dressed in her holiday sweater and jeans, her silver bob combed. I, however, am still in my flannel pajama pants and an OC sweatshirt, my hair piled into a messy bun.

"Thanks." I scoop more batter onto the griddle. "Do you think we have enough for everyone?"

"With the way the boys eat? Never. I'll mix up another bowl of batter."

My mind drifts to last night's gingerbread-house competition. Drew's smug grin grated on my nerves when his team beat ours by a handful of points. Then he slung an arm over my shoulders. "Better luck next time, Aud."

I rolled my eyes and brushed his arm away. But I didn't miss the way he eyed Jax when he did it. What game was he playing? He made it clear he doesn't like me like that. So why hate on Jax?

Drew's gloating reminds me of how Greyson used to act after demolishing me in pickleball games. Same cocky smirk, same unnecessary victory dance.

The kitchen door swings open, and my heart does a little skip when Jax walks in. His dark hair is sleep-tousled, but in a good way. He's wearing jeans and a T-shirt and dark-rimmed glasses I've never seen before. He looks...good.

He shuffles his feet before walking over to me. Then, in front of Mema, he wraps me in a hug, kisses my temple, and whispers, "I hope this is okay."

A surprised giggle escapes, and my cheeks flush. "Of course." Now, if I could only convince my racing pulse to calm down. My fake boyfriend plays the part well.

Thank goodness there's no mistletoe strung up over the griddle.

He releases me but stays close. "Good morning, Mrs. Davis. The pancakes smell amazing."

"Call me Mema, sweetie. Everyone does." She beams. "And you can thank Audrey for the wonderful smell. She's doing the cooking. I'm doing the mixing and slicing."

Jax rubs my back. "They look great. Can I help?"

"Sure." I step aside and hand him a measuring cup to use as a scoop. "You pour. I'll flip."

We ease into a rhythm, him pouring circles of batter while I tend to the cooking ones. When I flip one too enthusiastically and it lands half folded, we both laugh.

"Ah, man. I was doing great until I had an audience."

"Hey, it's still edible. Maybe."

I bump his hip with mine. "We can sneak it onto Will's plate. That's what he gets for showing us up in last night's decorating contest."

"Perfect. *Serve* him right."

I groan at his pun. But Will disassembled his group's gingerbread house, found a sharp knife to cut the pieces, and reformed them into a surprisingly awesome Star Wars AT-AT robot.

Show-offs.

While Mema runs out to the garage fridge, we chat about how Jax liked sleeping in the loft and the upcoming day. Working beside him feels natural and comfortable. There's none of the nervous energy I started feeling with Greyson, always worried I was talking too much or not enough. With Jax, the silence doesn't need filling.

I watch his profile as he dollops a perfect circle of batter. The slight furrow between his brows, the way he bites his lower lip in concentration. I've always thought he was cute, but here, in the golden morning light of Mema's kitchen, he looks…different. Annoyingly attractive.

I clear my throat as I try to clear my thoughts. "I've never seen you in glasses before."

"Yeah. I don't wear them often. I prefer contacts, but I was lazy this morning."

"I like them. They look good on you."

His lips curve into a bashful half smile. "Thanks."

I reach across the griddle to grab the syrup. Rising on my toes and leaning into Jax, I place a hand on his back for support.

House shoes shuffle in the doorway where Emma and Lucy, still in their pajamas, watch us. Emma's eyes narrow at my hand on Jax. Lucy can't stop smiling. Her hands clasp under her chin like she's watching her favorite romantic comedy.

I narrow my eyes at them and step away. "Morning, sleepyheads. Breakfast is almost ready."

"I see that." Emma flashes a smirk.

Mema bustles over with a stack of plates and napkins. "Good morning, dears. Will you please arrange the breakfast buffet?"

They grumble, but do her bidding and disappear from the kitchen.

I shake my head. Little sisters.

Mema wipes down the counter. "Greyson, honey, you're in for a treat tonight. It's the annual Carlton Landing Christmas bonfire."

"That's, um, an interesting tradition."

She chortles, turning to clean the sink, her back to us. "It's unique. That's for sure. Now, what's your major again? Audrey mentioned it, but my old brain can't keep track."

"Exercise Science."

I whip my gaze to Jax. That's *his* major. Not Greyson's.

His eyes widen when he realizes his mistake. My gaze darts to Mema as she begins to spin back toward us. Will she contradict him? I open my mouth to intervene, but she moves on, not noticing. "So, how did you two meet? What? What's wrong?"

Jax smiles, not missing a beat. "Oh, nothing. I dribbled some onto the power cord." He points, and sure enough, he's made a mess.

"Oh, don't worry about that." She wipes the cord with her rag. "There. Like new. So, tell me how you met. When's the first time you laid eyes on Audrey? Don't skip any details."

That was a close one. Romance magic to the rescue.

Jax pours another blob of pancake batter. "I met Audrey at the beginning of this year. I'd seen her last year at some of the freshman mixers, but we'd never talked or been introduced. Our first real conversation happened at the coffee shop on campus."

"Ah, I love a good coffee-shop romance! Go on."

"I was going there to meet my anatomy study group. I was running late, so everyone was already there. And who was curled up on the other end of the couch from my friends?" He pauses to nudge my shoulder. "A beautiful girl with wavy brown hair and deep-brown eyes."

Great. I'm blushing.

Mema giggles. She leans on the counter, not even pretending to slice fruit anymore. "What then?"

Jaxton dollops out another circle. "I made myself comfortable right between her and my friend Myles. Eventually, Audrey and I started talking. She was also there to work on homework with some friends. But since she's a brainiac, she was already done."

I roll my eyes and grin. "You didn't have much homework either since you spent so much time talking to me over the next hour."

"Oh no, I had homework. I blew it off to talk to the cute girl in the coffee shop. I had to stay up late that night finishing everything."

He chuckles, intent on the griddle, and I gawk, stunned.

Is that true? Did he stay just to talk to me?

Did he think I was…cute?

No. That's crazy. It's simply a part of our fabricated story.

Mema practically swoons. "What happened after that?"

"Well, we kept talking. We talked about nothing. Everything. It turned out we had friends in common. We both ordered another coffee, and when we got them, someone from the student paper came over and took our photo. They were probably working on a piece about The Brew. I wonder if they ever printed it."

"So then you asked her out?"

"Oh no. Not yet. The timing wasn't right. Right after that, my roommate and a group of our friends came in. Audrey seemed to like my roommate, so I stepped aside, though I was disappointed."

Mema slaps a hand on the counter, good-naturedly. "Audrey! What's wrong with you?"

I honestly don't know. "Um. I didn't know how he felt."

Jax lifts a shoulder and swallows. "Well, I made the wrong move. But when the time *was* right, I asked her out, and we went on our first date."

"Where did you go?"

"We caught a movie, and then went to Andy's for ice cream and a long walk around campus."

So…at what point did Jax's story veer into fiction? Or did it all have a layer of fiction over it? We never went on a date, but we did meet at the coffee shop. And later, Grey came in and introduced himself, squeezing in between us and taking over the conversation as he often did. And Jax scooted away.

How much of his story is true? I can hardly ask right now.

I squeeze his arm. "And the rest is history."

"How sweet." Mema sighs. "Well, I'm glad you finally got your girl."

Jax's gaze meets mine over the sizzling griddle. His voice is low. "Yeah. Me too."

The pancake I'm tending starts to smoke. I slip the spatula beneath it and flop it over, revealing a charred underside. Burned. I'm as good at flipping pancakes as I am at keeping track of this fake relationship.

23

Audrey

After breakfast, Mema announces we have free time and lunch on our own until two thirty, at which time we need to meet at the beach for the next competition.

Everyone heads in different directions. Will challenges Mema to a game of checkers. Morgan curls up on the window seat with her Christmas romance novel. Bryson claims the dining table for a game of Settlers of Catan and waves Jax and others over. Jax squeezes my hand and joins them.

Emma grabs her purse and camera bag from the hook by the door. "Want to see if the shops are open? I need to find a gift for Bryson's grandma."

Maybe. I need a distraction to take my mind off Jaxton and our supposed meet-cute. "I'm in."

Lucy bounds in from the kitchen. "Me too!"

Ten minutes later, we're bundled in coats and walking along the quiet streets. The wind off the lake nips at our cheeks, but the bright winter sun has me sliding my sunglasses on.

"So…" Lucy links her arm through mine. "Jax seems nice."

"He is."

"Like, really nice. And he's cute. And he looks at you like you hung the moon. It's adorable, actually."

I roll my eyes. "He does not."

"He totally does," Emma admits. "Especially when you're not looking."

"Guys, it's all an act. And it's starting to feel muddled as it is. Don't make it worse."

"I knew it! You like him."

"I can't like him. He and I have to break up in like two days. Everyone thinks he's Greyson. We can't bounce back from that."

My stomach tightens. This lie, which seemed simple enough, is becoming more complicated. It's starting to feel…oppressive.

We continue down the boardwalk and find rows of pop-up shops open for business. An event called Christmas on Water Street is well underway. Throughout the day, there will be craft stations, music, Airstream food trucks, and other fun activities.

We meander around until Emma finds the gift she was shopping for, and Lucy blows the last of her allowance money on a scarf.

An hour later, I get a message from Jax.

Jax: I lost the first round and decided to take a walk. Now I'm lost.

I chuckle.

Me: How can you be lost? This place is minuscule.

Lucy sidles next to me, still adjusting the knot on her new scarf. "Everything okay?"

"Jax went exploring and is now lost in the tiniest town ever. I should go find him."

She smirks. "That's right. You should. Maybe a romantic walk down the boardwalk?"

Will she ever stop?

Jax: Hey, it was dark when we arrived. I'm not sure which house it is.

Jax: Or street, for that matter.

Me: Tell me which intersection you're near, and I'll find you. I wanted to show you around anyway.

He does, and I pocket my phone. My sisters are watching me.

"What?"

Lucy crosses her arms and taps her foot on the wooden planks. "I was thinking. If you like him, it won't matter if you *act* like you like him. He'll think it's an act. You would have to *tell* him. And maybe you should."

Surprisingly, Emma doesn't protest.

I kick at a pebble. "I don't even know how I feel. And what if everything I'm confused about is also an act? What if he only sees me as his roommate's pathetic ex?"

"You never know until you put it out there." Lucy nudges my shoulder. "And I rarely consider you pathetic."

"Thanks, little sis. That's helpful." I leave my sisters huddled on the boardwalk, probably planning how they'll spy on us.

Minutes later, I locate Jax near the community garden. He's a lone figure meandering by the frozen, brown plants, hands in his jeans pockets. He must've opted for contacts, because the glasses are gone. Wind ruffles the dark hair sticking out from under his baseball cap.

"Found you." I step onto the sidewalk to join him.

His dimple folds into his cheek when he turns my way, and my stomach does that little flip-flop again. And no one is around. There's no one to perform for. That smile is for me.

"My hero." He nods toward the center of town. "So this is where little Audrey Blackwell spent her summers?"

"And Christmases and fall breaks. Lots of memories were made on these streets. Mostly on bikes."

"Sounds like a dream."

"It really was. And still is." I grab his jacket sleeve and pull him along. "Come on, Jaxey. You've got to see Water Street."

"Sure thing, *Cupcake*. Let's go find that Christmas magic."

We walk past quaint houses with their wide porches, every inch decorated for Christmas. Then we pass the pool and the bocce ball courts. Along the way, I point out other landmarks from my childhood, and Jax listens, asking questions and laughing at my adolescent mishaps. Conversation flows between us. No awkward pauses, no feeling like I need to impress him. Just…easy friendship. And something else, something electric that makes my skin tingle every time our hands brush.

Don't dwell on it.

We stop in the Meeting House for sandwiches before hitting the pavement again. I shiver when a gust of wind tunnels along the sidewalk, and Jax stretches an arm over my shoulders like it's the most natural thing in the world. "Let's get coffees."

"Perfect."

Though he protests, I pay since he bought our lattes two days ago. We wander toward the lake where I grew up waterskiing. Since Jax's family is originally from Colorado, they're more into snow skiing than waterskiing.

"I was probably six the first time I tried it." He blows across the opening in his coffee lid.

"Were you any good?"

"I was great in snow school with the other kids, but the first time my parents took me up to do an easy run, my mom went ahead to video Dad and me getting off the lift. I lost control and plowed right into her. Somehow, as Dad tried to stop me, he got tripped up too. It ended in a pileup."

The image of little Jax in his cumbersome snow gear flits across my mind. I hook my arm through his. "Hopefully, you didn't break any bones."

"Nah." He sighs. "I miss it. Who knows when I'll get to ski again?"

"You need to try a new adventure in Hawaii."

"My brother and I are taking surfing lessons."

"Jealous. I've always wanted to learn. You'll have to tell me about it when you get back."

He meets my gaze. That's not something a fake girlfriend would say. She wouldn't make plans to talk after the so-called breakup. Especially if they weren't friends before.

My cheeks warm. "I mean, if you want to. You could send a video of one of your epic wipeouts."

A grin spreads over his handsome face. "Oh, I'll tell you about it. And I'll brag about how good I was on my first try."

I shake my head. "We'll see."

We crest the grassy hill, brown at this time of year, that leads down to the beach. Hudson and Ava walk hand in hand along the sandy shore. Ava waves as we emerge into view. Jax and I raise a hand in response, and when we lower them back to our sides, he threads his cold fingers with mine. He steps closer as we stand shoulder to shoulder, facing the water. "Didn't even flinch. You're not bad at this acting thing." He watches me from the corner of his eye, almost like he's gauging my reaction.

I lean my head on his shoulder. "Well, that's because it's starting to feel pretty normal."

"Yeah?"

His lips quirk up, but there's also a hint of something else. Something like hope, which has my voice coming out softer than I intend.

"Yeah."

24

Audrey

A whistle erupts behind us. I pivot. Mema is lowering two fingers from her mouth as she bustles toward us.

"Oh, good. You two are here." She cups her hands around her mouth in Hudson and Ava's direction. "Snowman contest in five."

Hudson responds with a thumbs-up.

I peek at my phone. Huh. It's almost time. I lose track with Jax.

He pulls me along, and we stumble down the hill. When we reach the rocky barrier near the beach, he releases my hand to jump up onto one of them. "So we're building snowmen out of cold, wet sand?"

"Pretty much. And Mema will take away points if anyone complains."

"Brutal."

Over the next fifteen minutes, my family and neighbors gather to claim spots down the man-made shore, some grumbling, some laughing, and others attempting to sabotage their opponents' efforts.

When Emma swipes a handful of smooth stones Mom brought from the house for her snowman, she rushes to hide behind me.

I lean away. "Don't drag me into this."

"I got her phone too." Emma giggles, sliding it from her pocket. When Mom notices they're gone and stalks our way, Emma sends a FaceTime call from Mom's phone to mine, causing the Darth Vader theme song to play.

Everyone cracks up at this.

Even Mom. "Audrey Dianne, you still haven't changed my ringtone?!"

"I will. I will."

"You've been saying that for *four* years!"

This only makes everyone laugh harder.

Eventually, Emma returns the contraband, and Mom rejoins Dad in the sand.

When Drew arrives, he has no choice but to plop down in the space Mema reserved right next to Jax and me, since they're partners.

Awesome.

Aunt Suzanne, who has brought her snowman container—for what, I don't know—plants a hand on her hip. "Hey. No cheating, Drew. We all start at the same time."

"That's true," Mema says. "Sophia, stomp out that pile he's making."

The ten-year-old runs over and stomps Drew's head start into nothing.

Jax chuckles.

Drew scowls and then transforms his expression into something pleasant. "Sorry, Mrs. Davis. I didn't know." He winks at me as if I'm in on his ruse.

Jax stiffens, and I turn away from Drew. "Ignore him. He's being weird."

"Right."

When Mema gives the go-ahead, Jax and I start shaping what better form a snowman and not a lumpy blob.

Jax pats at the sand. "How big does it need to be?"

"Not big. Otherwise, it won't work."

"Any seashells out here?"

"I don't think so. We could use rocks for eyes. Sticks for arms."

"Good idea. I'll find some."

After Jax walks away, Drew flicks sand onto my jeans. "Remember when we buried Hudson in the sand?"

I form a head on top of our blob. "Yeah. And then we made him into a merman. I don't think it was as fun as he thought it would be."

Mema shakes her head and rakes sand with a toy shovel. "I made him rinse off in the cold water hose before coming inside to shower."

I giggle. "That wasn't the only time you made people rinse off in the water hose."

Drew smooths around their snowman's base. "Will today be one of those days?"

"You never know."

He gets back to work.

Still grinning about Hudson the merman, I find Jax watching me from across the beach. My smile falters when his answering one doesn't reach his eyes. Once he returns, he drops to his knees and lets the rocks he found tumble to the foot of the snowman.

I pick one up. "You okay?"

"Yeah, I'm good." He sighs and nods toward Drew, his voice low. "If you were hoping to make him jealous, it's working."

What? "That's not what I was hoping. Besides, he's always like that. Friendly one minute, ignoring me the next." I lift a shoulder. "It's nothing new."

Jax presses a twig into the sand for an arm. "I hate to say this because you two have a history and all, but he reminds me of Grey. Flirting with another girl when his girlfriend isn't around. And right in front of me."

"Greyson used to do that?"

"Sometimes."

Embarrassment flares hot in my belly, and I angle my cold cheeks away from him and toward the smooth lake. Grey really is a jerkface.

"I'm sorry." Jax nudges me. "I shouldn't have said that."

"It's okay. I needed to hear it."

"But hey, I mean, people change, right?" He nods at Drew. "Maybe he's realizing how great you are and what he's been missing all this time. What matters is that you're happy." He presses a pebble where an eyeball should go. It falls to the ground like his words. "This is impossible. Anyway, all I meant was if you brought me here to get his attention, we've done our job. We're good actors."

The word *actors* hits harder than it should. But he's right. That's what this is. A show. A performance.

I toss the fallen pebble at him. "Yep, great actors. And besides, I was thinking *you're* the one like Drew."

He brushes sand from his pants, giving me a look. "Don't insult me, Blackwell. How so?"

From the sand blob next to us, Mema calls the one-minute warning, so we move faster, adding smaller pebbles to complete the face.

I grab the cap from Jax's head and place it on the snowman. "I seem to remember *you* as the one who was friendly one minute and then ignored me the rest of the semester." I give him a lighthearted smirk. Point, Audrey.

But his hands pause over the mouth he's forming from a twig, and his smile slips.

Mema stands, and a burst of cold air hits us from across the lake. "Twenty seconds!"

I shiver, and Jax's hair rustles in the wind.

He starts to run a hand through it, but remembers his fingers are covered in sand.

I take the twig and arrange the snowman's mouth.

He flattens his hand and smooths the area around our little sandy snowman. "Audrey, I didn't ignore you when it was convenient or because I thought you were too young or in my way. I'm not like him. I didn't shower you with attention one minute and then ignore you the next. I stayed away from you because…" He pauses like he can't find the right words, then gulps. "Well, let's just say I had a crush on the girl who was dating my roommate. I *had* to stay away."

My gaze snaps to him, but he doesn't meet my eye.

"Time's up!"

I startle, glancing up at Mema.

I move my hands to my lap as a ragged breath rushes past my parted lips.

Jax lifts his head and meets my gaze.

He had a crush on…*me*?

25

Jax

Sand clings to my shoes as we walk back from the beach, the taste of our sixth-place snowman victory barely registering. My mind keeps replaying my confession.

Her expression said it all. Shock. Confusion. She'd been floored when I broke character and confessed something real. Why would I blurt that I had a crush on her the entire time she was dating my roommate? What was I expecting? That she'd say, "Yay. I was madly in love with you too. We should date!"

Idiot.

And yet, as we walk along the boardwalk back to Mrs. Davis's house, Audrey closes the distance between us and slips her hand into mine again.

Her fingers, cold and gritty from the December air and stray grains of sand, fit perfectly between mine. Is she holding my hand to keep up the charade for her family? To make Drew jealous? Or…because she wants to?

How can I decipher the truth with all the pretending we've been doing?

Her gaze flicks my way. "Good job on the snowman. The hat did the trick."

"Don't forget your sunglasses. They added a nice touch."

She adjusts them on her nose with her free hand. "They did, didn't they? We make a good team."

"Yeah, we do." I squeeze her fingers, testing the waters.

She squeezes back. What am I to make of all this? The easy connection we shared today feels strained, but maybe it's easing. Or is it all an act?

I wiggle my cap from my back pocket and shake it out. "Where do you think we stand after taking sixth?"

"Far down the list. The same couples seem to be winning everything."

Maybe, but what I want to know is if we're ahead of Drew.

"Is the Yuletide Challenge over now?"

"Oh no. Mema has a whole evening of smaller challenges planned. It should be fun. And exhausting. Are you up for it?"

"You bet."

We fall back into silence. Ahead of us, Emma and Bryson lean close, whispering about something, their shoulders bumping as they walk. Behind us, Drew is talking to Mrs. Davis, and when I tip my head, I catch his gaze slide toward Audrey. Just what is his endgame? Does he hope to win Audrey…from me?

I try to push the questions away. Seeing her laughing with him earlier when I wasn't around made me wonder what she wants. When all the pretending drops away, does she want to be with him?

For now, I'll let her take the lead. If she wants to talk to Drew, I won't stop her. I'll play my part as her fake boyfriend. And, of course, I plan to beat Drew in this ridiculous competition. It's easier than figuring out what's happening here.

The boardwalk gives way to a sidewalk that leads to Mrs. Davis's house. We trudge up the steps to the wraparound porch, and Mrs. Davis kicks off her boots. "Leave your shoes and all the sand outside! Hot cocoa's in the kitchen. The Challenge resumes in fifteen minutes."

I balance against the doorframe and toe my shoes off. "Wow, you weren't kidding. She runs a tight schedule."

Audrey chuckles. "She's been working on this for months."

After shedding our jackets in the entryway where Audrey yanks me out from under a cluster of mistletoe, we grab mugs of peppermint hot cocoa and settle near the fireplace to warm up.

Mrs. Davis is back to business in no time, waving her clipboard. "First up, holiday-crossword-puzzle race!"

Audrey's parents take the lead in that one. After that, we move into the brainteasers, and the next hour becomes a blur of holiday-themed riddles, word scrambles, and picture puzzles.

When the mental challenges end, Mrs. Davis ushers us to the dining room, where she twirls a handful of scarves over her head. "Blindfolded gift wrapping! Ladies first! Men, you can direct your partner if needed. We'll judge by speed and technique."

Audrey and I grab our supplies and find a place to sit on the hardwood floor. I tie a scarf over her eyes. Leaning in, I whisper in her ear. "I hope you don't need directions. I'm not much on gift wrapping."

She faces me, our faces inches apart. "I'll be fine. But should I be worried about your turn?"

"Um. Maybe."

She smiles, not seeing as I watch her mouth below her blindfold. The urge to close the space between us surges, so I sit back before I do something stupid.

Audrey wraps the gift with ease. When she's done, it's almost perfect. My only contribution was to say, "The tape is to the right of your knee."

"How did you do that? It's perfect."

She pulls the scarf from her head, fixing me with those deep-brown eyes. "I love wrapping gifts. I always volunteer to do it for everyone."

Too soon, Audrey's tying the blindfold over my eyes. Then her warm breath moistens my ear. "Be honest," she whispers. "How bad will this be?"

Goose bumps, hidden under my hoodie, erupt over my arms. I turn toward her, my voice low. "Well, I've helped my mom wrap presents before. Actually, I think I watched."

She giggles, but doesn't move away. Is she thinking the same thing I was earlier? "Oh boy. We're doomed."

Footsteps draw near, and the chatter around the room dies down. Mrs. Davis's voice calls out over us. "Ladies, quick now, give your man a smooch—sorry, Drew, none for you—and get ready to begin."

Audrey's intake of breath is mere inches from my cheek. I don't move a muscle.

Will she kiss me?

Mrs. Davis's footsteps move away. Can Audrey get away with skipping it if she wants?

But she still hasn't moved.

Are we under the mistletoe, and Mrs. Davis has pointed it out?

Audrey's fingers brush my cheek, and my heart rate ticks up a notch.

And then…her lips are against mine.

I kiss her back for the briefest moment before she scoots away.

It wasn't a long kiss, but it wasn't abrupt either.

Her thumb circles my cheek one more time before her hand drops.

Neither of us says a word.

Mrs. Davis gives the countdown, and Audrey tucks a cardboard box into my hands.

I'm supposed to have the mental capacity to wrap a present *now*? After that?

She's right. We're doomed.

When I've finished, after following Audrey's directions—"fold the paper over, no, not like that, now tape that corner, good"—the final product could've been wrapped by a toddler. It's gotta be the worst wrapping job in the room.

Mrs. Davis tries not to laugh when she comes by to judge it. "How many pieces of tape did you use?"

"I don't know, like ten."

She giggles, marking her paper, and walks away.

I elbow Audrey. "How many did you use?"

"Three, of course. That's the only acceptable number."

While Audrey helps Mrs. Davis tally the scores, I haul my knee up and drape my arm over it. I look up. Am I sitting under mistletoe?

I'm not. So why did she kiss me?

Mrs. Davis announces that Audrey's uncle Clint and aunt Emily have pulled ahead to take the lead, followed closely by Hudson and Ava. Everyone else falls below, including us, but we're leading Drew and Mrs. Davis by three points, so I'm happy.

After that, we hang out in the living room while we wait for our pizza order from Mama Tig's. I want to bring up the kiss to see what Audrey says about it, but the opportunity doesn't come. When the pizza arrives, she rushes to help set everything out, leaving me propped against the couch next to Emma and Bryson.

Bryson pitches his voice low. "So…things seem to be going well."

"Yeah, I think so. I mean, we're pulling it off okay."

"That's not what I meant."

Across the room, Drew maneuvers to stand near Audrey in the pizza line. He says something to make her smile, and I look away.

"It's fine. I'm having fun."

Emma scowls in her sister's direction. When Audrey returns, pizza in hand, she asks, "What were you and Drew talking about?"

Audrey picks up a slice of pizza. "Oh, we were reminiscing about the neighborhood Olympics. Remember, he and I won two years ago."

She shrugs, but I see what he's doing. Drew is reminding her that the two of them work well together…and she'd be his partner right now if I weren't here. Is that what she wishes had happened? But what about the kiss?

All part of the act. Right?

After everyone has had their fill, Mrs. Davis claps her hands. "Get ready for the real competition," she announces, eyes twinkling. "Head-to-head challenges!" She unfurls a poster board with an elaborate bracket system sketched out in colorful markers. My name, well, Grey's name, is paired with various family members for different activities. We'll fly solo for these challenges, but each couple's points will be combined. Oh, good. I face Drew in cornhole near the end of the bracket. Nothing like standing shoulder to shoulder, tossing bags at a hole to settle the awkwardness.

My first match pits me against Ava in ladder ball. She destroys me, wrapping the bolas around the top rung with scary precision.

Ava's husband, Hudson, pats me on the shoulder. "Don't feel bad. She beats everyone."

My next challenge sends me to the garage for a game of Ping-Pong against Audrey's uncle Clint. Here, my dorm skills pay off. I win handily, earning points back for our team.

I move on to my next competitions, and through it all, I keep track of Audrey, who's engrossed in her own matches, winning horseshoes against a cousin and narrowly losing a heated Mario Kart race to Emma.

The Yuletide Challenge takes us all over the house and property, and even up the street to the bocce ball courts and back again. Despite the December chill, everyone's energized by the competition, cheeks flushed as holiday lights reflect in eager eyes.

As twilight descends, I head to the backyard for my final match, cornhole against Drew. He's already there, sorting the red beanbags from the blue. We'll keep score, playing only two sets.

Drew tosses a red bag over his head and catches it. "Three points in the hole, one on the board, and zero for everything else. Ready to lose—*Greyson*?"

What's with the strange emphasis on my borrowed name? "We'll see."

We take our positions next to each other, facing the wooden target. We're alone in this corner of the yard.

Drew tosses the first bag, landing it cleanly in the hole.

"Three points." He steps back to allow me to square up with the board. "You know, I heard the weirdest thing today. I don't normally listen to private conversations, but I couldn't help myself. This was too good."

My bag lands short of the board, and an uneasy feeling settles in my stomach. "Oh yeah, what was that?"

The smirking Drew lands another bag near the hole. "One point. Emma and Bryson were talking about you. At first, I didn't care to listen—it wasn't my business— but when I heard the words *fake boyfriend*, I thought I'd better make it my business."

I freeze, my bag halfway through my toss. If this is all he has to go by, he might not know much. I swing my hand back again and toss the bag, sinking it into the hole. "What are you talking about?"

"So I did some digging. I checked out the only Greyson that Audrey follows on Instagram." He tosses another perfect shot. "Guy doesn't look anything like you."

I lift my palms. "I don't like Instagram." It's true. I don't. Let him think I don't have an account.

"That's the weird part, though. I found *your* account. Unless you have an identical twin or something. But I don't think so, do you…Jax?"

Oh, this is not good. He knows. And what will he do with the information? I toss my last bag, and it lands in the grass.

"And the best part?" Drew gloats. "Audrey doesn't even follow you. I found you by sorting through the real Greyson's followers. So I'm guessing what I heard is right. You're not dating Audrey. You guys weren't even connected before this little trip to Carlton Landing."

He strides toward the board to retrieve our beanbags, and I suck in a long breath.

Oh man. What now?

There's no denying anything, so what am I supposed to do?

When he returns, tossing the blue bags at my feet, I say, "Look, don't tell anyone. I can explain—"

"No need," Drew interrupts, his tone casual but eyes cold. "Your turn. And I get it. Audrey needed a fake boyfriend to save face or to get my attention or something, and you stepped in. Very noble."

"It's not like that." I toss a bag, and it slides down the board and onto the ground.

"No?" He lands another shot. "I've known Audrey since we were kids. She's had a crush on me practically her whole life."

Arrogant much? I raise a brow. "And she told you that?"

"She didn't have to." His confidence grates, though, based on what I've heard, he's right. His next words are even worse. "And I should thank you. It took you being here for me to realize how great she is. What I'm missing out on. And I'm so glad to find out the thing between you isn't real."

A muscle ticks in my jaw, and I let another bag fly. It thuds on the board. This guy has some nerve. "That's up to her, isn't it?"

Drew's smile never wavers as he takes aim. "Actually, she already told me she can't consider a relationship with me while you're around. Something about what her family would think." His bag flops in the hole.

My chest tightens. Is that true? "Drew, don't tell anyone about this. She'll be humiliated." I overshoot my next toss.

"I don't plan to. But she doesn't need you here anymore. I'm here for her now. You need to leave. Let Audrey figure out what she wants. And I won't tell anyone about your ridiculous arrangement if you go."

His last toss is a perfect shot. "Game. I win. Big time."

He walks away without looking back, leaving me staring after him, mind racing. Did Audrey say that?

Either way, I need to tell her what Drew knows so she's not blindsided.

When I return to the house, everyone's bustling around, zipping jackets, and heading out the door.

I stop Bryson. "What's happening?"

"Mrs. Davis said she'll announce the final scores after the bonfire since we're running behind." He claps me on the arm. "Bundle up. Let's go."

I head upstairs and to the loft to grab my cap. By the time I'm back on the landing, the house has mostly cleared. Voices from the kitchen have me padding down the stairs in my socks.

"…would have been unstoppable if we'd been partners."

"I doubt that, Drew. You and I have always had our wires crossed."

It's Audrey and Drew.

"I mean it," he says. "And maybe it's time we uncross all those wires. We've had some good times over the years, haven't we? Remember our fun last summer?"

"Yeah, but—"

"I know what you're going to say," he cuts her off. "And, Aud, I'm sorry for the way I treated you once everyone showed up. I was a world-class idiot. I didn't then, but I finally see you now. Truly."

She's quiet. When she speaks, her voice is soft and breathy. "Drew…"

"What are you two doing? Let's go, or we'll miss it." It's a man's voice. One of the uncles?

I pad back up the stairs before I'm caught eavesdropping. The front door opens and closes, and I climb up the ladder and sink onto the beanbag chair in the middle of the room.

I knew this would happen. Never go for a girl who's recently broken up with someone, or worse, who's still into an old flame. Why would I put myself in the position to be the rebound guy? Again.

I shake my head.

Drew is right. If I make myself scarce, Audrey will give him a chance. It's what she's always wanted. And if she doesn't give him a chance while the opportunity is here, she might always wonder.

And so would I.

I like her a lot, but I'm not who she wants to be with.

She told me this was fake, and I knew that going in. That's why I can't be mad at her. She didn't do anything wrong.

Sure, something seemed to spark between us. But it was all a part of the show. We're good actors after all.

And now…Well, I want her to be happy.

The front door opens, and footsteps pound up the stairs.

I grab my duffel bag and start shoving my things inside.

26

Audrey

I put a step between Drew and me, forcing a casual smile as I gesture up the boardwalk, where everyone's heading to the Christmas bonfire. "I should catch up with my family."

"Sure." His smile never falters. "But we should hang out more before we leave town. Maybe tomorrow?"

"Maybe." I'm already backing away. "I'll see you at the bonfire." I jog up the boardwalk until I'm well away and then slow my pace. His words echo in my mind—"I finally see you now"—and I'm not sure if they make my heart flutter or sink.

I zip my jacket to keep out the crisp December air and pull my scarf tighter around my neck. The path ahead is dotted with people making their way toward the grassy landing, where the Christmas tree-shaped bonfire will soon light up the night. I scan each cluster of holiday sweaters, jackets, and knitted hats. No Jax.

I lost track of him during the final set of challenges. Now, with Drew's sudden interest rattling around in my brain, I need the steadying presence of my fake boyfriend by my side.

The path opens onto Water Street, which has been transformed for tonight's festivities. String lights crisscross over the Airstream food trucks, one of which is serving free popcorn and hot cocoa. Live holiday music drifts from the stage down the street. Children dart between adults, some clutching glow sticks that leave trails of neon in the gathering darkness.

And there, at the top of the grassy hill separating the street from the sloping lawn that rolls down to the beach, is the awaiting wood-plank tree. The massive structure's built from scrap lumber and arranged in the shape of a towering evergreen. It must be twenty feet tall, a testament to the community effort and holiday spirit of Carlton Landing. People circle it, taking photos and claiming spots for the best view.

But no Jax.

Emma is at the front of the hot cocoa line, so I intercept her once she has her drink. "Hey, Em. Have you seen Jax?"

"I thought he went ahead with you." She blows across the steaming cup.

"No, I was—I got stuck talking to Drew."

She raises an eyebrow. "Huh. What'd you talk about?"

I wave the question away. "I'll tell you later. Listen, if you see Jax, tell him I'm looking for him."

"Okay. Bryson went back for gloves. I'll ask if he saw him."

I continue my search, moving through the crowd, past families, excited children, and couples huddled close against the cold. The air smells of pine and cinnamon, with undercurrents of woodsmoke and chocolate. Any other year, I'd be soaking in the magic. Tonight, my thoughts are a jumbled mess.

Drew's sudden interest has me reeling. As I walk the circumference, I admit what I've been avoiding: maybe I did want to make Drew jealous. Maybe deep down, that was the whole point. But now? Now I'm not so sure I want that at all.

"Audrey!" My dad waves from across the circle, beckoning me over.

I make my way, finding most of our family gathered here.

"Where's Greyson?" he asks.

"I don't know. I can't find him."

Dad extends an arm around my shoulders. "He'll turn up. Hard to miss someone setting a giant Christmas tree on fire."

I nod, but…should I go back? Did we leave him?

The circle around the bonfire continues to fill in.

Emma sidles next to me. "Look!" She points up the hill where two guys are running this way down the boardwalk. Bryson and Jax. Emma shakes her head. "Finally. Nothing like the last minute."

The boys don't see us in the growing darkness, so we push our way toward them. Jax's gaze meets mine. There's something in it, hesitation, maybe, that makes my heart stutter. He smiles, but it doesn't quite reach his eyes.

I squeeze in next to him, facing the tree. "I couldn't find you. I thought you were ahead of me."

"Sorry. I had to take care of something." His gaze strays across the circle, and I follow it. Drew is glaring in our direction. Is he…angry?

Emma and Bryson exchange a look I can't quite decipher.

Something's wrong. I thread my arm through Jax's, drawing closer to his side. "Are you okay?"

He glances down at me, his gray-blue eyes reflecting the twinkling lights. "Audrey, there's something I need to tell you—"

"Audrey. Emma. You know we stand together as a family. Come over this way." Mema's voice cuts through whatever Jax was about to say.

We obey and shuffle back toward Dad. As the bonfire is lit, I feel Drew's glare from the other side.

All heads turn toward the structure. At first, only a wisp of smoke rises from the bottom, but soon, a dark-gray tornado of smoke spirals from the openings between the wood planks and up into the sky. Soon, the tree begins to glow from within. The flames crawl upward, and heat pulses in waves, warming my face despite the chill in the air. The wood crackles and pops. The flame grows and spreads, sending sparks dancing into the night sky.

Children gasp in delight. Phones lift to capture the spectacle.

And my hand slides down Jax's arm until I thread his fingers with mine. "Pretty cool, huh?"

"Very cool." Golden light dances across his face as he stares up at the flame. Eventually, though, his gaze strays toward Drew again. This time, Drew's head bends while he speaks with his parents. Mrs. Edwards breaks away from their group and approaches my mom, her features creased. She leans in, saying something that makes my mother's expression lose her festive joy. I imagine Jax pulling away, though he hasn't moved.

I tug on his hand. "What's going on?"

The firelight casts forlorn shadows across his features. He squeezes my fingers and pitches his voice low. "Grey wasn't right for you. Find someone who is. Don't settle. Please."

My stomach drops. "What are you talking about?"

The bonfire roars behind us, crumbling the structure into an unrecognizable black heap.

His lips dip toward my ear. "Drew knows I'm not him."

My eyes go wide. "What?"

"He told me right before we came here. He also told me I should leave and give you some space to figure things out."

I shift back, gaping. "When did he—"

"I don't have a car, and I didn't want to get an Uber without saying goodbye first." His gaze flicks to where Drew's mother is still talking to my mom. "He told me he wouldn't tell, but from the looks of it, he has."

Heat flares in my chest. He's telling on me…like we're elementary kids. "He doesn't get to decide when you go or when you stay."

Jax's sad smile stops me. "It's okay. Everything will be fine. I mean, we succeeded, right? We made him jealous. We made him notice you. That's what you wanted all along, right?"

The words sting, peppering me with small kernels of truth. But they're also wrong.

"Jax, that's not what this was all about."

"Again, it's fine. I understand. I want you to be happy. And Drew is coming around."

I shake my head, struggling to find the right words, but Jax silences them when he brushes strands of hair behind my ear. "And why wouldn't he?" His fingers linger on my cheek. "You're fun and smart and beautiful." His hand drops to his side. "He's realizing what an idiot he's been."

I'm aware that my mother is stalking toward us as the world slows. I half expect the Darth Vader theme song to play. The roaring bonfire, the crowd, the music, it all fades to background noise. Because I'm staring at a boy who has bent over backward for me. He's been thoughtful and attentive. He bought me the perfect birthday gift. He endured my crazy family and went along with everything.

He makes my heart soar.

But we've made such a mess. And it isn't real.

My heart has nowhere to go but right back down to earth, where everything is about to crumble like the blackened tree behind me.

Jax spots my mom and squeezes my fingers one more time. "Everything will be okay. This is your chance to figure out what you want."

"Jax, wait—" My words are cut short as his hand slips from mine.

"Audrey Dianne Blackwell." Mom crosses her arms, shooting a wary glance at Jax. "We need to talk."

27

Audrey

Mom steers me toward Mema's backyard, her hand firm against my elbow after a silent walk back to the house. The smell of woodsmoke clings to my hair and clothes as we step onto the porch away from curious onlookers. Dad follows, and the porch light casts harsh shadows across their faces, highlighting his confusion and Mom's pinched expression.

I wrap my arms around myself against their scrutiny. The lie that seemed so necessary days ago has morphed into something outrageous and childish.

What was I thinking?

Mom spins to face me. "Explain yourself, young lady. Nancy told me Greyson isn't who you say he is. And that's not even his na—"

Dad stops her with a hand on her shoulder. "Let her talk, honey. Audrey, is it true?"

I nod, my shoulders slumping. I force the gathering tears to stay hidden away. I've always been a crier when someone is disappointed in me, even now, when I'm almost twenty. "Yes."

Dad lets his arm drop from Mom's shoulder. He was giving me the benefit of the doubt, assuming it wasn't true.

Mom pinches the bridge of her nose. "I would never expect this kind of irrational behavior from my oldest child. You're so responsible. Why would you lie about something like this? To us? To Mema in her home?"

A lump forms in my throat, and my toes curl in my boots. I duck my head and focus on them. "I'm sorry. I don't know. It *was* irrational. It was a terrible idea, and I'm sorry I lied."

"You told us you were dating Greyson well before the end of the semester. Was that a lie too?" Dad's voice is gentler than Mom's.

I nudge a pebble off the porch. "No, I *was* dating Greyson from my chemistry class. We were together for about two months. But he, um, he dumped me. Last week. Very publicly in the cafeteria on campus. I was humiliated."

Mom's expression softens. "Oh, Cupcake. Why didn't you tell us?"

"Because of this." I gesture around us. "The Yuletide Challenge. Mema was so excited about making it a couples' thing this year. And then Drew was bringing his new girlfriend, and they were involved in the Challenge. Everyone would be asking me where Grey was. Emma even told me some of the cousins had already said they thought I made him up after I first said he couldn't come. I don't know. I—" I swallow hard. "I panicked."

"So, who is the boy upstairs packing his bags?" Dad points toward the loft window. "And how did you talk him into this?"

"His name is Jaxton Harrison. Jax. He's Grey's roommate. I've known him all semester, though not well. I tutored him the week before his chemistry final. He heard me freaking out about my situation. He felt sorry for me. Plus, his parents were snowed in in Colorado, and his mom was forcing him to attend this wedding in Guthrie by himself. I could tell he didn't want to and was sad about spending the first days of Christmas break alone."

"So you did go to a wedding? That was real?"

"Yes. I was his date to the wedding."

Mom shakes her head. "And with all of these problems, you thought pretending—lying—was the solution?"

"I didn't think at all. *That's* the problem. I wanted to avoid the questions, and I didn't want to retell the humiliating breakup story all weekend. I didn't want to be the only one without a significant other for the Yuletide Challenge."

Dad rubs his forehead. "Audrey, you have to know—none of us cares if you're single. In fact, as your father, I prefer it."

"Dad!" The word bursts out of me. "If that's true, then don't let Mema plan a couples-only Christmas. If that's true, don't let her invite the boy I've had a crush on since I was a kid. Especially if he's bringing his perfect new girlfriend."

They're quiet until Mom says. "Okay. I see your point. But it's not an excuse for lying to the whole family. You could have told us you were uncomfortable with it. Your mema loves you. She would've scrapped the whole thing."

I pick at my jacket cuff. "I know. You're right. But it felt too late. She'd already worked so hard on it."

"You could have brought Grey—I mean, Jax—as a friend."

"Maybe. But…" I lift my head. "Please don't blame him. Don't be mad at him. He was trying to help me. He's played with the kids, helped with dishes, made pancakes, and been a good sport. He's been nothing but respectful and considerate to everyone."

"Except for the lying, of course."

I frown. "Yeah, except for that."

The back door opens, and my heart sinks as Jax steps onto the porch. Bryson is right behind him, followed by Mema. Jax has his duffel bag slung over one shoulder, and he's holding his jacket instead of wearing it.

Curious faces peek out the back windows.

Jax's face is composed, but his eyes, those gray-blue eyes that crinkle at the corners when he laughs, are filled with resignation and something else. Disappointment, maybe.

He faces my parents, and I should step between them to shield him from their disapproval. But his voice is steady when he speaks. "Mr. and Mrs. Blackwell, I want to apologize for everything. I'm so sorry for deceiving you. It was never my intention to disrespect you or your family traditions. I'm not sure what got into us. My name is Jaxton, and I'm a sophomore at OC like Audrey. She tutors me in chemistry, which she's good at, by the way."

Despite everything, the corner of his mouth lifts, and a matching smile tugs at my lips. A tear falls down my cheek. His fingers move like he might brush it away if we were alone.

"I take full responsibility for my part in this." He turns to Mema. "I'm sorry for inserting myself into your family Christmas, Mrs. Davis. But I did have a good time." He lowers his chin toward his shuffling feet. "Well, up until now. And I enjoyed meeting all of you. I don't have a big family like this. It was…nice."

Mema studies him, her head tilted to one side. "I forgive you, young man. Audrey seemed to enjoy your company. But thank you for the apology. It means a lot." She pulls him into a hug he wasn't expecting.

When she releases him, she addresses my parents. "We worked it all out inside. Jax's parents flew into Oklahoma City this afternoon, and they're driving to meet Jax and Bryson halfway. I told him he could stay, but under the circumstances, he's understandably ready to get going."

Sophia bursts from the back door. "Wait! I finished your present." She rushes to Jax and holds out her palm, exposing a dark-green clay-bead bracelet. "It's green like mistletoe, your favorite."

He lowers to one knee and takes it from her. "I love it. Thank you, Sophia."

When he stretches it onto his wrist, she beams and then dashes back inside.

Bryson jingles his keys. "Ready?"

Jax nods, his forlorn gaze on me.

Dad clears his throat. "We'll wait here while you walk him to the car to say goodbye."

We walk down the porch steps side by side, not touching. The gravel driveway crunches under our boots as we head toward Bryson's dad's truck. Everyone's gazes follow us, both from the porch and through the windows.

Bryson reaches the truck first, so he slips inside and starts the engine. The exhaust creates puffs of white in the cold air.

"I'm so sorry for all of this," I say.

Jax's lips tuck into a sad smile, causing his dimple to appear. "I was glad to spend the weekend with them. And with you." He shakes himself from the serious mood. "And remember, I'm the one who came up with the idea in the first place. You should blame me."

"No way. It was a joint effort."

There's so much I want to say. About how this started feeling different somewhere along the way, about how I don't care what Drew thinks anymore, and about how, for some reason, despite everything, I don't want him to leave. But with my family watching and Bryson waiting in the car, all I can manage is a pathetic, "Text me when you get home safely, okay?"

He nods, his lips parting, and inhales a breath like he might say more. But everyone's still watching us.

"Bunch of eavesdroppers," I grumble.

He laughs and opens the door. "I'll talk to you later."

An unfamiliar ache tightens my chest as I grip the doorframe. "Have fun in Hawaii."

He slides in. "Bye, Audrey."

"Goodbye, Jaxton."

And then he shuts the door, and I step back as the truck pulls away from the curb. My family remains on the porch, silhouettes against the warm light. I don't want to return to them yet. I stand alone in the driveway, shivering against the cold, as I track the red taillights until they disappear around a bend in the road.

An arm wraps around my shoulders, and a tear rushes down my cheek.

Mema thumbs it away, her usual twinkle back in her eye. "So, at what point, exactly, did you fall for that boy?"

This only makes me cry harder.

28

Audrey

I clutch my pillow to my chest, alone in the bedroom I'm sharing with Emma and Lucy. A melancholy Christmas song whines over my Bluetooth speaker. I've refused every knock on the door until my family decided to leave me in peace.

My cheeks feel tight from dried tears, and my thoughts won't stop spinning between Jax's abrupt departure, my lips on his earlier this evening, and the words *fun and smart and beautiful*. Oh, and of course, the enormous mess I've created.

At what point did I fall for him? Mema's question hangs in the air like the lingering scent of her peppermint perfume. Do I have the answer? Did I fall for Jax?

My phone buzzes against my thigh. I ignore it. But when it buzzes a second time, curiosity gets the better of me. I fish it out of my pocket, hoping it's from Jax, though he's likely in the car with his parents and almost home by now.

But it's not from him. It's Drew's name on my screen.

Drew: Hey, Audrey, sorry about what happened with what's-his-name. Want to get dinner tomorrow night?

Drew: As in, a real date this time.

Drew: It's about time, don't you think? *Wink emoji*

I stare at the messages, reading them three times. My adolescent dream, delivered via text message. Drew Edwards wants to take me on a real date. The same Drew who "sees me" after years of invisibility. The same Drew who told Jax to leave so I could "figure things out."

I drop the phone onto the bed without responding and flop back onto the mattress, hugging the pillow again.

Any other time in the last six years, I'd have been elated.

I close my eyes. Where's the excitement for getting the full attention of my childhood crush? Instead, Jax's face as he stood on the porch, duffel bag slung over his shoulder, storm-gray eyes resigned, runs through my head.

A knock at the door, this one louder.

"Audrey?" Mema's voice. "Are you ready to talk yet?"

"Fine." I cover my face with the pillow.

The door clicks open. "Well, that's good, because I was coming in anyway." She pulls the fluffy lifeline from my grasp, and I find not only Mema but a small army of female concern. Mom, Emma, and Lucy, all wearing variations of the same worried expression, surround my bed.

"Can we join you?" Mom sounds gentler than during our confrontation.

I sit up, making room for their invasion. Mom and Mema perch on the edge of my bed, Lucy flops next to me, and Emma sits cross-legged at the foot.

"We wanted to check on you." Mema brushes a tangle of hair from my face. "We were worried."

"I'm fine." I haul the pillow back into my lap. "Mostly embarrassed. I'm so sorry I lied."

Mom takes my hand. "Cupcake, we forgive you, of course."

Lucy nods. "We do. I mean, it's not like you had Jaxton pretend to be a doctor and do surgery or something. Borrowing his roommate's name is fairly tame as far as deceptions go."

Mom glares at her. "Anyway, the point is, we want you to stop torturing yourself up here and come back down to be with the family. Everyone makes mistakes."

Lucy picks at a blanket hem. "I don't think that's the only thing bringing her down."

"Definitely not," Mema says.

Mom bounces her gaze between them. "What do you mean?"

I bite my lip and reach for my phone. I open the text from Drew, hand it over, and then bury my face in the pillow again.

There's silence as they read it, although the deep chuckle of men's voices carries up the stairs from where they play another board game.

"I don't understand." Mom shifts, jostling the mattress. "Isn't this good news? You've liked that boy for ages."

"Oh, Mom." Emma finally speaks. "Catch up! She doesn't like him anymore. She's fallen for her fake boyfriend."

I emerge from the pillow. "I haven't. I can't."

Lucy giggles. "You totally have. You might even be in love with him."

Heat creeps up my neck. "I *can't* like him. He's my ex-boyfriend's roommate. And the whole thing was fake. Anything I've felt was based on a lie. He was pretending. I was pretending."

Emma tries not to smile. She fails. "That blindfolded kiss when you thought no one was looking didn't seem fake."

My mouth drops open. "Emma!" I swing the pillow, and she blocks it with her forearms, laughing.

The corner of my mouth starts to turn up, but falls. "Jax left. And he knows I've always liked Drew. But… even then, wouldn't he have stayed if he liked me? Wouldn't he have fought for me?"

Emma snorts. "He assumes you want to be with Drew."

"Do you?" Mom studies my face. "Want to be with Drew, I mean?"

"No! Even though it's what I've always wanted. He's finally—*finally!*—asked me out. I should be thrilled. Instead, I feel awful. Why?"

Emma lifts a shoulder. "Um, because he's a jerkface?"

"Emma. No name-calling." Mom shakes her head, but Emma's words trigger something in my brain.

That's what I've been calling Greyson since he dumped me.

Drew and Greyson.

They both flirt with other girls when their girlfriends aren't around. They only want to be around me when it's convenient for them, and now, they've both publicly humiliated me.

Jax was right. They are alike.

I groan. "I'm such an idiot."

Mema rubs my back. "No, you're not. Love is complicated."

"I don't deserve it. I should never be allowed to like anyone again. Drew, Grey, and now my fake boyfriend." I bop the pillow over my face again and again. "I always choose wrong."

Lucy steals the pillow, hugging it to her chest. "But are you sure Jax is *wrong*?"

A new knock interrupts our conversation. Emma opens the door to reveal Bryson, who's just returned from delivering Jax to his parents.

"Hey. Sorry to interrupt." His gaze finds me in the room full of women. "But Jaxton gave me this to give you." He lifts his palm to reveal a small wrapped package.

"What is it?" My voice rasps my throat. I stare at his offering like it might bite me.

Bryson shrugs and sets the package on the bed.

With trembling fingers, I untie the red string and unfold the paper. I open the black box to reveal a bracelet made from tiny, pale-green stones. The bracelet I admired during OC's Lighting of the Commons. The brushed-gold accents catch the lamplight, gleaming against the dark-colored box.

"Oh." Moisture gathers at the corners of my eyes.

"What is it?" Mom scoots in.

"It's a bracelet. It's from the Christmas market at school. I mentioned that I liked it. But…that was last week. Before all this started." I free it from the box. "Bryson, do you know when he got this?"

"No idea. But he had it with him, so it had to be before you came here."

"He must've bought it that night without me knowing." I rub my thumb over the stones. We'd been shopping together, and he was wearing that awful sweater. He'd come to my rescue with Mom over FaceTime as the song "What Are You Doing New Year's Eve?" drifted in the air. Jax must've been paying attention when I showed him the bracelet. I didn't know.

Emma clears her throat. "I don't mean to state the obvious here, but that boy likes you too."

Bryson crosses his arms. "Oh, for sure."

My gaze snaps to his, eyes going wide. "He told you that?"

"Well, no. He didn't have to."

"But he still left."

"Because he assumed that's what you wanted." Lucy shakes the pillow at me. "He thought you wanted to see where things would go with Drew."

Emma loops her arm through Bryson's. "And don't forget he did say he wants you to be happy. This is what he assumed would make you happy."

"Well, he was wrong." My fingers close around the bracelet, the stones warm from my touch.

"Obviously." Emma rolls her eyes.

The bracelet's tail ends sway, a pendulum to and fro like my thoughts. "What if we're wrong? What if it was all an act?"

Mema steals it from me, slides it over my wrist, and clips it in place. "Well, that's a risk you have to take."

The stones sparkle, though nothing like they did under his Christmas sweater lights. It cuffs my wrist, a tether to him. "He's about to leave for Hawaii. He won't be back until the twenty-eighth."

"What are you going to do?" Emma asks.

I chew on my lip as a breath bottles in my chest to mix with a slew of butterflies. "I have an idea."

29

Jax

I drag my suitcase from the back of the car, muscles aching after the overnight flight from Hawaii. On this New Year's Eve, Oklahoma's winter chill feels like a slap after over a week in paradise.

My carry-on slips from my shoulder. I don't have the energy to adjust it. All I want is to get in the house and relax on the couch. But my mind keeps drifting to Audrey. What's she doing now? Is she still in Carlton Landing? Is she with Drew? Is she happy?

Dad and my brother, Michael, haul more bags from the trunk, their usual efficiency hampered by jet lag and the extra three days we added onto the end of our trip.

When my neck pillow falls to the dirty garage floor, I pause and huff out a breath that forms a cloud in the air, so different from the tropical warmth we left.

Michael trudges past me, his tan more pronounced than mine after a week of surfing lessons. "Move it or lose it, little brother. The sooner we get everything inside, the sooner I can crash. I want to nap before Jessie comes back from her parents to ring in the new year."

He and his fiancée have planned a quiet celebration here at the house with Mom and Dad since we're all travel-tired. I'll be the fifth wheel since I don't have anything else to do.

Super.

The house smells inviting and familiar, and I kick off my shoes next to my cubby in the laundry room.

"Last one." Dad slides the final suitcase inside the door and closes it on the cold. "I'm making coffee."

Mom's not in the living room to order us to take everything to our rooms, so I flop on the couch next to Michael. A week in Hawaii is supposed to leave a traveler rested. Instead, exhaustion weighs me down.

The trip was amazing, though, like Audrey said, even if there wasn't any snow. The surfing lessons with Michael. The luau where Mom and Dad embarrassed us by attempting to hula. The sunset cruise. Christmas morning in our condo, where Jessie couldn't stop smiling at the Number One Sister ornament Audrey helped me pick out for her. I'd thought it was lame, but

Audrey convinced me Jessie would love it since she's an only child and I don't have any sisters. She was right.

Michael reaches for the remote. "So… what are you going to do about that girl you like?"

I told my parents the bare minimum after Bryson dropped me off that night. That I'd pretended to be Audrey's boyfriend for a family holiday, things got complicated, and it was over now.

Over the weekend, my parents were curious about this mystery girl I'd taken to Zoe's sister's wedding. Of course, Mom had heard all about it from Mrs. Holt. But as the story unfolded, they'd been disappointed I'd presented a fake relationship to their friends and appalled by my rash decision to lie to an entire family during their Christmas get-together. Which is fair, now that I've been through it.

When I recounted the events to Michael on the flight to Hawaii, he picked up on the fact that I like Audrey more than I should. I've assured him our situation is hopeless, but he disagrees.

"Her name is Audrey," I respond now. "And I'm not doing anything. I told you. She's into some other guy. Besides, the time in Hawaii helped me forget her. I'm over it."

Michael snorts. "Dude, you've been checked out all week. Not even surfing on those baby-sized waves could get you to focus. You're *not* over it."

I snatch the remote from his fingers and turn on the TV. "They weren't baby waves. The instructor said I was a natural."

"The instructor says that to all the tourists." Michael sinks deeper into the couch cushions. "Okay, walk me through it. I need more details. She asked you to be her date to her family Christmas. You agreed. What then?"

"Well, actually, it was my idea. I offered. She said no at first."

"Huh. And she was dating your roommate before that?"

"Yep."

He cuts his gaze my way. "And how long have you liked this girl?"

I flop my head back onto the couch. "Too long to be acceptable."

He chuckles. "I knew it. I knew you wouldn't offer to be her fake date unless you liked her."

"Whatever."

"Sounds like you've got a mess on your hands."

"Why couldn't it be simple? We were helping each other out. The wedding was easy, but things got complicated in Carlton Landing. When we got there, I realized she wanted to make that other guy jealous. And it worked. By the time I left, he was begging for a chance with her."

"Simple? You agreed to spend an entire weekend pretending to be the boyfriend of a girl you like. That has disaster written all over it."

"Yeah…well." I refuse to voice the words *you're right.*

"Well, did she say she was giving this other guy a chance?"

"No."

"And you just…what? Left her to be with him?"

I pick at a loose thread on my jeans. "What was I supposed to do? Make a scene? Confess my feelings? Tell her I've liked her since the beginning of the semester?"

"Yes, you should have."

"And ruin her chance with the guy she's wanted since forever? Besides, he figured out our whole fake relationship anyway. Said he'd keep quiet if I backed off."

His eyebrows shoot up. "Wow. Sounds like a real charmer."

"Right? Don't get me started."

"Jax, you can't give up. You don't even know what happened since you left."

"I know, but everything was so confusing when I was there. All the things I was feeling were based on something fake. How could I tell what was real?"

"Well, maybe Audrey felt the same way. Maybe she wasn't sure what was real either. Maybe she thought *you* were faking. And that makes sense because that's what you told her you were doing."

I tilt my head back on the cushions, glaring at the ceiling. He's right. I need to figure out what to do. But that little voice in my head keeps warning me against a girl who might still be into a guy from her past. Zoe taught me all I need to know about that.

Mom's voice cuts through our conversation as she appears in the doorway, a laundry basket braced on her hip. "Can you boys take your things up before you settle in? Michael, you're in the guest room. Oh, and, Jax, there's a package for you." She props the basket on the back of the couch and hands me a padded envelope. "The neighbors brought in the mail. I found it by the back door."

I take it, turning it over in my hands. "Thanks, Mom."

"Now, up! Luggage to your rooms." She hauls the basket to the laundry room as Michael and I extract ourselves from the couch. He grumbles something about Mom turning his old room into a gym.

Since we both moved out, Mom has grown accustomed to the house being decluttered, and she doesn't tolerate our messes as much as she used to. We climb the stairs past all the old photos on the wall.

Michael hefts his suitcase one stair at a time. "This conversation isn't over. I still think you're being an idiot."

"Thanks for the support," I mutter, veering toward my bedroom.

Inside, I drop the suitcase, close the door, and survey the familiar space. My high school basketball medals still hang from a nail next to the bookshelf, though now they dangle alongside college textbooks—including chemistry, which, thanks to Audrey, I scored the B I needed. The walls are a patchwork of old movie posters, and my OC sweatshirt hangs from my desk chair, right where I left it before leaving the mainland.

I flop onto the bed, still holding my mail. I lift it over my face to read the return address. It's from… Eufaula, Oklahoma. The nearest city to Carlton Landing.

I sit up.

My heart ticks up a notch as I tear open the package and reach inside. Maybe I left something.

Inside, nestled in crumpled newspaper, is a bronze disk on a red-and-green Christmas-themed ribbon. The medal reads, "8th place, the Yuletide Challenge." I run my thumb over its embossed pine tree. Eighth place. Wow. That's terrible. But did we at least beat Drew and Mrs. Davis? Not that I care. And why would Audrey send me this? Surely, she'd want to keep it.

Beneath the medal lies a note on holiday stationery. Audrey's neat handwriting covers the page. I swallow hard before reading.

Jax,

I hope you had a great time on your trip. I can't believe you spent Christmas in Hawaii! I'm writing because I wanted to show you our medal. Eighth place isn't that great, but we did narrowly defeat some people, including my parents and Mema. Ha.

Yes! Take that, Drew.

> I've also included a photo I found. I thought you would like to see it.

I reach back into the envelope and pull out a photograph. It's the photo the school newspaper reporter took on the day Audrey and I met. We're sitting close together, smiling, holding up our steaming coffee mugs. Others are visible around us, but with the way we're leaning in, they might as well have not been there at all. She must've pulled this from their website and had it printed. I flip it over. On the back is another handwritten message.

> It was a good day. I knew you were someone I could like from the moment you sat down. But then you disappeared.

This is…the first photo we ever took together.

I place it next to the medal on my comforter.

Audrey sent me the same kind of package Mrs. Davis sent Audrey's grandpa. The ribbon they'd won together in the three-legged race. The first photo they'd ever taken together, with a note on the back. And what had she been saying?

"I wanted to be subtle. Hint that I wanted him to come back without putting too much pressure on him."

She liked him. She wanted him to come back. But she wasn't sure he wanted the same. Is that what Audrey is saying? It has to be. Why else would she send these exact things?

But…Mrs. Davis had also given him a hint, along with a time and place to find her.

> Anyway, I'm sorry for the way we had to leave things. Maybe we can talk soon.

> We plan to enjoy Carlton Landing at least until the new year. New Year's Eve is usually pretty chill. In the afternoon, we'll attend the festival, and dinner will be at 6:00. It's always delicious. I bet you would like the apple pie.

> Love, Audrey

I hop off my bed, tripping on the rug. When I right myself, I fumble the time onto my phone.

No, no, no.

Six o'clock on New Year's Eve has come and gone.

I sink onto my mattress.

I should have gotten this message days ago, but we extended our trip.

She thinks I stood her up.

30

Audrey

I trail behind my family on the boardwalk, my boots dragging against the weathered planks as leftover Christmas lights still twinkle around doorways and along rooftops. The night air bites at my cheeks, sharp and clean. The scent of lake water and chimney smoke drifts in the air. My phone burns a hole in my coat pocket where I've checked it seventeen times in the past hour. Still nothing. No missed calls, no texts, no indication Jax even received the package I sent him last week.

Maybe I was too subtle. Maybe I should have spelled it out—"Come back on New Year's Eve." But my message, the photo, the medal…it wasn't *that* subtle, was it? I know the package arrived because I tracked it. And I know they were planning to come home three days ago.

Ahead of me, Mom links arms with Mema while Dad carries a folding chair and a thermos of hot chocolate. Emma and Bryson walk close together, their fingers entwined between them as they laugh about something. Even Lucy is more animated than usual, chattering to her best friend, Ian, about the musicians booked for Carlton Landing's Porch Fest this spring. The two of them are already opening a package of sparklers, a December 31 beachside tradition of ours. Everyone's caught up in the New Year's Eve energy—everyone, except me. I'm hunched into my winter coat, hiding from the wind and people.

I pull out my phone again, the screen's blue glow harsh against the warm golden light strung along the boardwalk. Still nothing. My fingers hover over the keyboard. Should I send a text to say, "Happy New Year"? Or maybe, "How was your trip?" But what then? "Oh, and hey, did you get my awkward attempt at recreating Mema's romantic gesture?"

No. Absolutely not.

The disappointment I've been gathering all evening sits heavy in my chest.

Six o'clock—*Maybe he's running late.*

Seven—*Maybe he ran out of gas.*

When nine came and went, I faced the truth. Either he didn't understand my message, or worse, he wanted to pretend I didn't put it out there in the first place.

I dim the screen. Stop agonizing over it. It's fine. Maybe everything is happening as it should. If nothing else, Jax showed me I don't need to settle for anyone who isn't right for me. Even someone I had a crush on for too many years.

I finally spoke to Drew Sunday afternoon, the day after Jax left. We'd all been to church and lunch and back home. I was walking to the blue mailbox in town, my stuffed padded envelope tucked under my arm. In the process of second-guessing every word of the letter, I nearly dropped it when Drew appeared out of nowhere. He must've spotted me leaving Mema's house from his window.

"Audrey, wait up." He jogged down his porch steps to catch up.

I stopped, clutching the package to my chest. "Oh. Hey, Drew."

"You never responded about dinner tonight. Did you see my text?"

Heat crept up my neck. "I saw it."

"And?" His smile was confident, expectant. The same smile used to make my heart race. Now it makes me tired.

"And I don't think it's a good idea." My words are steady. "Thank you, but no."

His expression shifted. "I don't understand. I thought that's what we've both been waiting for. For the fake boyfriend to move on, so we could give this thing that's been building between us for years a try. Admit it, it's what you've always—"

"Drew," I cut him off, surprising us both with my firmness. "I need you to listen to me, okay? Yes, maybe that's what I've wanted for a long time. I would have given anything to have Drew Edwards ask me out. But I see now that you knew I liked you all that time. You encouraged my crush when it was convenient for you, but you ignored me when it wasn't. You broke my heart over and over again. And now, when you thought I wasn't available, you decided you wanted to ask me on a date."

"That's not—"

"It is. And even if it wasn't, the truth is, Drew, I don't trust you. I can't. You never made me feel like I was worth your time. And my heart has moved on. I like someone else now."

The words hung in the cold air between us, and I couldn't believe I stood up to him. Drew's mouth gaped open as if the possibility that I might prefer someone else never occurred to him.

"The fake boyfriend?"

"His name is Jax. And you outed him to everyone. You mortified both of us."

"I'm sorry, but I thought I was doing the right thing. For us."

"Drew, nothing about the weekend was the right thing. No next step would have been right. I shouldn't have lied to everyone. You shouldn't have gotten involved. It was a disaster all around. I'm not mad at you. I forgive you, and we can still be friends. But it will be different now."

I haven't seen Drew since. His family left Carlton Landing that evening, deciding to spend Christmas at home instead of extending their stay through the New Year. I'd watched their car disappear down the winding road and felt only relief.

"Aud!" Emma's voice cuts through my brooding. She and Lucy have doubled back to where I'm dragging my feet along the boardwalk. "Come on, slowpoke. You'll miss the sparklers."

Lucy loops her arm through my left one while Emma does the same on my right. They tug me across Water Street and onto the sloping lawn leading down toward the manufactured beach.

Lucy nods at my phone, still clutched in my fingers. "Anything?"

I shake my head.

Emma bumps my shoulder. "I'm sorry, Aud."

"It's okay. It was a long shot anyway."

The sandy shore stretches out before us, dotted with my bundled family members. Aunt Suzanne and Mema have spread a blanket with snacks and noisemakers on top. New Year's Eve in Carlton Landing is a small affair. Most renters leave town after Christmas, so there's only the annual dinner for anyone who's left and no community party at midnight. However, our family created its own tradition. For those of us still around, we like to ring in the new year at the beach. Sometimes it's too cold or windy, but when we can, like this year, we build a campfire and bring sparklers.

Several of my younger cousins, who don't usually stay up this late, are already racing around with sparklers, leaving trails of golden light in the darkness. Dad helps Uncle Bob with the fire, Mom sets out marshmallows and roasting sticks, and Lucy runs ahead to help light the sparklers.

As our boots sink into the sand, I shake myself.

Have fun. It's New Year's Eve. And before me, a new year with new possibilities.

Lucy presses a lit sparkler into my hand, and the golden sparks cascade toward the sand, warm and bright against the December night. I smile as it hisses and pops in my grip. Before long, we're all enjoying the moment, spinning circles and writing our names in trails of light. I let myself get caught up in the simple joy. The way the sparks reflect in Emma's delighted eyes, the concentration on Lucy's face as she attempts to write her name fast enough to see it all at once, the squeals from the younger kids.

When the sparklers burn down to nothing, I plop in the sand next to Lucy.

"I'm sorry, Connor had to leave."

She lifts a shoulder. "He was in a mood. He's always in a mood. It's nice to have Ian around, though."

I nod. "Best friends are like that." We watch him pretend to chase Sophia with the smoking end of his sparkler. She shrieks while he sneaks glances at Lucy.

As always, Lucy is oblivious to the fact that her bestie has a crush on her.

Just when I open my mouth to inform her, he runs over to join us, along with Bryson and Emma.

"So…" Bryson leans back on his elbows. "New Year's resolutions. Anyone have a good one?"

Emma crosses her legs at the ankle. "Not me. I can't keep them, so I don't make them."

"Come on." He nudges her. "Play along. I'll go first." He clears his throat. "I resolve to beat Emma at Mario Kart."

Emma snorts. "Good luck with that. I'm the master. And…I don't know. Exercise more? Or at all."

I pull my knit cap lower over my ears. "That's a good one."

Lucy and Ian give their answers before Bryson turns to me. "What about you, Audrey?"

"Hmm. I would also like to beat Emma at Mario Kart."

Emma tosses a pebble at me. "You can't recycle someone else's resolution! Even if it's true. Try again."

I dig my gloved fingers into the cool sand. "I want to be more truthful. With myself and with others. I only dated Greyson because I wanted to have a boyfriend.

He wasn't right for me, and I knew it. My roommate was right. I didn't want to be alone. I have to be honest with myself and not treat people that way because I don't want anyone to do that to me. To be with me because it's convenient or fits a mold. I also want to be truthful with others. I'm sorry, guys. I lied, and I dragged you into it. I guess I want to…be better."

The words feel heavier than I intended, weighted with memories. "Sorry, that was too deep. I'll go with that and winning the Yuletide Challenge next year."

Emma rubs my back. "Hey, it's okay. We forgive you. And for the record, you're already pretty great."

I look down at the sand. "Thanks."

We debate who's most likely to take first in the challenge next Christmas until Emma surges to her feet, brushing sand from her jeans. "Bryson and I are going to get some hot cocoa from Mema. You guys want anything?"

"I'm okay," I say.

Lucy and Ian shake their heads.

Soon, the sugary sweetness of roasted marshmallows wafts my way. Mom, Dad, and many others are huddled near the fire, roasting sticks in hand. Hudson and Ava cross the footbridge to the dock, their hands linked as they move in and out of the firelight. Morgan and Will have found a quiet spot on a rock outcropping, her head resting on his shoulder.

Well, at least I have Lucy.

But she pops up. "We'll be right back." She hauls Ian off to the dock.

I sigh. That's fine.

"Five minutes to midnight!" Hudson calls from the dock, his voice carrying across the beach.

The others begin gathering in clusters. Aunt Suzanne calls the girls in from where they were throwing rocks into the water. They move farther down the beach, readying more sparklers. Emma and Bryson carry their hot cocoa in the other direction.

I should join my parents at the fire. Soon, they're all moving down the beach away from me. I hug my knees to my chest and gaze out over the water, which reflects the campfire's light in dancing ripples. The cold seeps through my jeans, making me shiver. There's something peaceful about this. It's a new beginning with new possibilities. In minutes, it will be a new year. A fresh start.

Footsteps squish behind me. Lucy must've come back.

The ground shifts as she settles in the sand, close enough that her warmth presses into my arm. Long legs stretch out and then curl in to match mine.

Those...aren't Lucy's boots.

I turn, and my heart skips a beat.

I suck in a shallow breath.

"Jax."

31

Audrey

Jax's gaze is steady as he takes in my wide eyes, and the corner of his mouth lifts into a nervous and perhaps hopeful half smile. "Hey."

His voice is low as the distant glow of sparklers and bonfire light illuminates his face. Those gray-blue eyes that have occupied my thoughts for the past week now gaze into mine. His dark hair is messed, and sand clings to his boots.

I blink hard, convinced I'm hallucinating.

"Jax." My voice comes out as barely a whisper. I glance around at my family, who seem overly occupied with the sparklers.

"They know I'm here."

"What? H–how."

His shoulder brushes mine, solid and warm and real. He's close enough that I can smell the faint scent of his cologne. "I called Bryson after I got the package you sent."

My heart hammers against my ribs. "I wasn't sure you'd gotten it."

"I didn't…until today. We stayed in Hawaii longer than planned. I got home about four hours ago."

"What?!" Dark circles spread under Jax's eyes, and I long to run my thumb over one. "You must be exhausted."

"Maybe a little. Sorry, I'm late. I left my house right after reading your letter."

"Four minutes to midnight!" Hudson calls out of the darkness over the water, mingled with the sounds of the crackling fire and distant laughter.

Jax adjusts his coat sleeve. "Or maybe I'm just in time?"

"Yeah. Just in time." I duck my head. "I didn't think you were coming."

He's here. He's really here, sitting next to me.

I meet his gaze again. "I'm glad you did."

"Me too."

"When you didn't show for dinner, I figured either you didn't get the package or you understood what I was saying and…" I look away over the inky water.

"Everything's been so confusing. I don't know what's real or pretend."

"I know the feeling." He's quiet, staring into the darkness, where moonlight creates a silver path across the water. "The thing is, I *was* pretending. But not in the way you think. I've been pretending for ages."

I frown. "What do you mean?"

He faces me fully. Sand shifts beneath us.

"I've been pretending not to like you since the first day we met." His voice is soft, barely a whisper. "When Grey showed up that day and I thought you liked him, I disappeared like you said. I had to. I liked you. A lot. I couldn't hang around the two of you, so I kept my distance. I was cold toward you. Rude, probably, and I'm sorry for that. But it was something I had to do. Self-preservation and all."

My breath catches. "Jax—"

"When I was assigned to you for tutoring, I should have asked to be reassigned. I knew it would make everything worse for me. But somehow, I just didn't care."

The words hang between us, heavy with months of unspoken truth. All those moments last weekend when it felt like more than pretending, that's because it was.

I clear my throat. "That first day, when you sat down on the couch in The Brew, I noticed you right away. And then we talked, and we laughed together. I thought you would ask for my number. But then your friends showed up, and I felt like I was in the way.

Probably, because *you* pulled away. I was…
inconvenient. And it was easy to feel that way, because
I've felt that way before."

His gaze shoots to mine. "That's the way Drew
always made you feel."

I nod, and he hangs his head, shaking it. "I'm such
an idiot."

"No, you're not. Everything between us has been
confusing. Jax, I liked you that day too. I didn't
understand why you stood aside. And then, I admit, I
spent months being mad at you for ignoring me."

He groans. "And now?"

I inhale, tasting woodsmoke and crisp December air.
"I guess you could say somewhere along the path,
maybe around the giant snowman and the killer terrier,
it started to feel less fake. Like it wasn't pretend at all. I
like you, Jax."

His gaze softens, eyes dancing with firelight. "I like
you too, Audrey."

From somewhere behind us, music starts playing.
Something soft and familiar that makes my heart skip. I
turn toward the sound as someone—Bryson, maybe—
takes off down the beach, leaving his phone and the
music on the rocks.

What in the world?

Oh. It's—

"Jax. This song. It's our song. Did you…plan this?"

He grins and lifts a shoulder as Ella Fitzgerald belts out her New Year's Eve song. "I learned from the original ladies' man."

I laugh. "Are you talking about my papa?"

"Of course."

"So…my family is involved in this?"

"Maybe."

I roll my eyes, and he shifts closer. "Audrey?"

"Yes?"

"Do you want to go on a real date?"

"Definitely." What a simple answer after all the confusion.

His smile could power the lake house. "Good. Because I was running out of romantic grand gestures to convince you."

"You drove two and a half hours on New Year's Eve after an eight-hour flight. I think you're good."

"I should mention I may have broken several speed limits getting here."

"Rebel."

I lean into him as he wraps an arm around my shoulders. His other hand reaches for mine.

"Jax, you don't even have gloves on."

"You think I had time to look for gloves?"

I take his hand, pressing his fingers between my hands. "So… now what?"

From the dock, Hudson's voice rings out again. "One minute!"

The rest of my family has gathered further down the beach, where sparklers create trails of light in the darkness. They're giving us space, their silhouettes clustered together, laughter dancing on the wind. What do my parents think of Jax's return? Mema will be insufferably smug about her romantic advice, and Emma and Lucy will demand every detail.

He studies our sandwiched hands. "Now, we figure out how to date for real."

"No more pretending. No more fake names. No more elaborate schemes."

"Jax and Audrey?"

I lift my chin. "Audrey and Jax."

The simplicity of it feels revolutionary. I scoot closer, angling toward him. "After all this, I figured we'd kiss in the mistletoe land mine."

He lifts a shoulder. "Too cliché for us. But I am wearing a handmade, one-of-a-kind mistletoe bracelet under this jacket."

My giggle slips free. "That's more like it."

Hudson and Ava begin the countdown, yelling from the darkness. "Fifteen, fourteen…"

I thread his fingers through my gloved ones. "Maybe we kiss at midnight. And not because we're pretending or because anyone expects it, but…because we want to?"

He angles closer. "I was thinking the same. But…"

"But?"

"Ten, nine..." The voices are louder now, more urgent. Sparklers hiss and pop in the distance. The end of our song grows louder.

"But don't make the mistake of thinking I didn't *want* to kiss you the other times. Because I did."

"Same." I wrinkle my nose. "Especially before your terrible wrapping job."

Our lips are centimeters from each other.

His dimple appears. "I knew it."

"Two. One."

And then his lips are on mine.

"Happy New Year!"

But only for a moment before a boom cracks overhead and I gasp. A shower of brilliant gold and silver blooms across the sky. We've never had fireworks on New Year's Eve before. Everyone claps and cheers, and the girls dance around with their sparklers.

Hudson whoops from the dock, lighting another one.

I return my gaze to a smug Jax.

"This was you too?"

"I might have suggested it would be cool if the guys found a place to buy some."

I pull him close again as another boom splits the sky. "Happy New Year, Jaxton," I breathe against his lips.

"Happy New Year, Audrey."

I thought I remembered what it felt like to kiss him, but this is different. More honest, full of promise instead of pretense. His arms tighten around me as more fireworks bloom above us, their light reflecting off the water in shimmering trails.

32

Jax

I shift my weight from one foot to the other, inching forward in The Brew's morning rush line. The coffee shop buzzes with students intent on caffeinating before their 9:00-a.m. classes. The barista calls out drink orders over the hum of conversation and the hiss of the espresso machine, and I check my phone. Fifteen minutes until Audrey's tutoring session starts. Plenty of time if this line keeps moving.

When I'm up, the barista, a girl I recognize from my psychology class last semester, nods. "Morning, Jax. What will it be?"

"A large caramel latte for me and a medium double espresso oat milk latte for my girlfriend."

The word *girlfriend* still sounds odd on my lips. After all the pretending and then being honest with each other, calling Audrey my girlfriend feels like a warm, fleece-lined hoodie that fits just right.

While waiting for our drinks, I scan the seating area for familiar faces. Charlotte, Audrey's roommate, who I now consider a friend, waves from a chair in the corner. Textbooks, notebooks, and highlighters surround her. Is she still studying for her history test scheduled later this morning? I wave back and then give her a double thumbs-up, mouthing, "Good luck."

She makes a face and tucks back into her books.

"Jax! Two lattes," the barista calls.

I grab the drinks, securing lids on both, and head out of The Brew, through the library, and down the quiet hallway to the private tutoring rooms. I've made this walk many times now. Last semester, it was to receive tutoring from Audrey, but now it's because I want to. Because I want to see her.

Her voice issues from the second room on the right. The glass door is ajar, so I stop outside, listening. She and her student haven't started, have they?

But she's alone, near the table and facing the other way, speaking in soothing tones. I pause, raising an eyebrow until Emma's voice rings out from her MacBook. She's on a video call.

"Mom acts like I've never been away from home before." Emma sounds both exasperated and fond. "I spent a whole semester away at Carlton Landing with Mema. But now that I'm on my own at OC, she texts every hour to make sure everything is good."

Audrey chuckles. Her hair is pulled up in a messy bun today, exposing her nape, where wisps have escaped. She's wearing that deep-green sweater that brings out the flecks of gold in her brown eyes. Not that I can see from here, but…I know.

"She's worried because you're on your own for the first time. When I moved in freshman year, she called me three times a day for the first week."

"Yeah, but you didn't have an older sister already at the same school. It's like she thinks I'm helpless without you hovering over me."

"I don't hover."

Uh-huh. She hovers.

"Sure. Sure," Emma says.

"Well. Imagine how it will go when Lucy moves out. The baby of the family. Mom might move in with her."

"Poor girl."

"It will get better. I promise."

I step forward, lurking in the doorway, the coffee cups scalding my fingers. Audrey's head turns, and her mouth stretches into a grin.

Emma notices. "Jax walked in, didn't he?"

"Maybe." Audrey doesn't take her gaze from me.

Wow, I've got it bad for this girl.

"Hey, Jax," Emma says.

I move in front of the screen to say hi, and the three of us make plans to meet for lunch since Emma's roommates will be busy at a study session.

After the eventful Christmas break at Carlton Landing, I've come to like Audrey's family. Especially Emma, who was the first to speak up for me when their parents were unsure whether their oldest daughter should date someone who would go along with such a crazy scheme. And they're right. It wasn't a good plan…though it did bring Audrey and me together, so I can't hate it too much.

Mr. and Mrs. Blackwell came around, though. I apologized again and have shown them I'm a decent person. Mema needed no convincing. She adores me for reenacting her late husband's romantic gesture. I don't want to brag, but I might be her favorite.

Emma hangs up, and Audrey closes her laptop, her look warm and inviting.

We sit next to each other at the small table, and I place her coffee on it and nudge it her way.

"For me?"

"Of course. I saw you check the line earlier. Figured I could brave the morning rush for you."

She takes a sip and closes her eyes. "Mmm. My hero."

I reach for her hand and thread my fingers through hers. "Guess what?"

"What?"

"It started snowing."

"Already!?"

I nod. "By this evening, there should be enough for a mini snowball fight, and by tomorrow, a snowman."

"Perfect. I'm glad you're getting some snow in your life."

"Finally. And we have to take advantage because by Thursday—"

"It will be gone. Got it. Any chance of sledding on the cafeteria trays?"

"I guess we'll find out."

I brush my thumb over the bracelet dangling from her wrist. The one I surprised her with for Christmas. "I'm glad you like this."

"It's my favorite."

I push loose hair from her cheek with my other hand, my fingers lingering on her face.

She laughs. "Careful. If you keep doing that, I might have to kiss you right here."

"That was my plan all along."

"Let's not forget I'm on the job." But she doesn't move away.

I tuck the strand behind her ear.

She leans in, and so do I. Our lips meet.

Until a throat clears from the doorway.

We jump apart like we were caught stealing, and I nearly knock over my coffee. A girl with a heavy backpack and a textbook clutched to her chest shuffles her feet in the doorway.

"Um, sorry." She shifts from foot to foot. "Are you Audrey? My tutor?"

Audrey smooths her hair, her professional demeanor returning despite the lingering pink in her cheeks. "Yes, that's me. You must be Melissa. Come on in."

This is my cue to leave, so I stand, gather my coffee, and plant a kiss on top of Audrey's head. "I'll see you at lunch."

Her gaze is soft as she meets mine. "See you then."

As I move toward the door, the girl steps aside to let me pass. "You guys make a cute couple."

I pause, glancing back at Audrey, who's watching me with that particular smile she reserves for me, the one that makes me feel like I'm the only person in the room worth looking at.

"Thanks," I say. "I think so too."

"It seems real." Melissa adjusts the textbook in her arms. "I mean, the way you look at each other. It's nice. Genuine."

I meet Audrey's gaze again. What a perfect observation after all the pretending, all the acting, all the confusion, then finally, the truth.

I wink, not looking away from her beautiful face. "That's because it is."

***

**WANT TO SEE PHOTOS OF THE REAL
CARLTON LANDING CHRISTMAS BONFIRE,
AND READ MORE ABOUT AUDREY AND JAX?**

Type this address into a web browser to check
out photos of Carlton Landing at Christmastime and an
opportunity to read a bonus scene!

Photos and **BONUS SCENE:**
www.evaaustin.com/bonfire-photos/

Read the other books in the My Favorite Color series:
My Favorite Color is Your Something Blue
My Favorite Color is the Golden Hour.
These books can be read in any order.

Dear Reader,

Thank you so much for reading this YA Christmas romcom! It means so much that you gave *My Favorite Color is Mistletoe* a chance.

Are you looking for more sweet romance books like this one? Me too! I'm always searching for books to suggest to my readers. Sign up for my newsletter, and I'll send book recommendations as I find them. (I'll also let you know when the next *Favorite Color* book comes out!) Visit evaaustin.com/signup/, and don't forget to follow me on Instagram.

If you have questions about this book, the next in the series, or writing, please email via the contact form on my website. I look forward to hearing from you!

- Eva

Acknowledgments

I want to thank my wonderful family for supporting me in my writing journey! Thanks to my husband for being my biggest encourager. You're the one who consistently asked, "What's your next goal?" or "Did you meet your goal today?" Thanks for keeping me accountable!

Thank you also to my kids for encouraging me and putting up with writing weekends and holiday editing. I love you so much and can't wait to see what God has in store for you!

Thanks to my editor, Deirdre. You tell it like it is, and I love it!

And a special thanks to Avery for answering all my questions about the Lighting of the Commons at OC.

Eva Austin is a fiction writer, author of contemporary novels for teens who want to be swept away in a fun, light-hearted, and sweet love story.

Eva holds a BS from the journalism and mass communication department of Abilene Christian University. She teaches digital art to high school students while also managing her blog, Book Series Recaps, and writing fantasy stories under the name Sara Watterson.

When not writing, teaching, or enjoying her kids' many activities, Eva likes reading on the back porch, drinking coffee, and hanging out with her super-cute hubby. She lives in central Oklahoma with her husband and three children.

Stay up to date by joining Eva's mailing list here:
https://www.evaaustin.com

Let's be friends:
https://www.instagram.com/eva.austin.author
https://www.goodreads.com/eva_austin

www.ingramcontent.com/pod-product-compliance
Lightning Source LLC
Chambersburg PA
CBHW032235310726

48973CB00008B/2149